D1020543

STEALING BRADFORD

OTHER BOOKS BY MELODY CARLSON:

Carter House Girls series

Mixed Bags (Book One)

Girls of 622 Harbor View series

Project: Girl Power (Book One)
Project: Mystery Bus (Book Two)
Project: Rescue Chelsea (Book Three)
Project: Take Charge (Book Four)
Project: Raising Faith (Book Five)
Project: Run Away (Book Six)

Books for Teens

The Secret Life of Samantha McGregor Series
Diary of a Teenage Girl Series
TrueColors Series
Notes from a Spinning Planet Series
Degrees Series
Piercing Proverbs
ByDesign Series

Women's Fiction

These Boots Weren't Made for Walking
On This Day
An Irish Christmas
The Christmas Bus
Crystal Lies
Finding Alice
Three Days

Grace Chapel Inn Series including

Hidden History
Ready to Wed
Back Home Again

carter house girls

STEALING BRADFORD

MELODY CARLSON

ZONDERVAN®

ZONDERVAN.com/
AUTHORTRACKER
follow your favorite authors

We want to hear from you. Please send your comments about this book to us in care of zreview@zondervan.com. Thank you.

ZONDERVAN

Stealing Bradford
Copyright © 2008 by Melody Carlson

Requests for information should be addressed to:

Zondervan, *Grand Rapids, Michigan 49530*

Library of Congress Cataloging-in-Publication Data

Carlson, Melody.
    Stealing bradford / by Melody Carlson.
      p. cm. -- (Carter House girls; bk. 2)
    Summary: DJ's efforts to make sense of Christianity, prayer, and the Bible only seem to make it harder for her to deal with the inability of the girls in her grandmother's boardinghouse to get along, especially after Taylor begins flirting with Rhiannon's boyfriend.
    ISBN 978-0-310-71489-7 (softcover)
    [1. Christian life — Fiction 2. Interpersonal relations — Fiction.
3. Boardinghouses — Fiction. 4. Grandmothers — Fiction 5. High schools — Fiction
6. Schools — Fiction 7. Conduct of life — Fiction 8. Connecticut — Fiction] I. Title.
    PZ7.C216637Ste 2008
    [Fic] — dc22

                                                      2008001421

Scripture taken from the New King James Version. Copyright © 1982 by Thomas Nelson, Inc. Used by permission. All rights reserved.

All rights reserved. No part of this publication may be reproduced, stored in a retrieval system, or transmitted in any form or by any means — electronic, mechanical, photocopy, recording, or any other — except for brief quotations in printed reviews, without the prior permission of the publisher.

Interior design by Christine Orejuela-Winkelman

Printed in the United States of America

09 10 11 12 13 14 • 25 24 23 22 21 20 19 18 17 16 15 14 13 12 11 10 9 8 7 6 5

STEALING BRADFORD

1

STEALING BRADFORD

"I'M SORRY, BUT MY CAR'S just not big enough for *all* the girls," announced Eliza as they were finishing breakfast. She pushed a glossy strand of blonde hair away from her face and then took a slow sip of coffee. As usual, Eliza was stylishly dressed, her hair and makeup absolutely perfect, and she looked ready to make her big debut at Crescent Cove High today.

"And I've already reserved my ride with Eliza," said Taylor a bit too smugly. She too was perfection—at least on the surface. But DJ was well aware that looks can be deceiving.

Eliza smiled at DJ now. "And I told Kriti she could ride with me too ... which only leaves room for one more." Eliza and DJ hadn't really spoken since last night when they'd made their splashy entrance into Harry's beach-house party together. A few hours and a lifetime later, DJ had left the party and driven all the girls (except Taylor and Eliza who weren't ready to go) back to the Carter House in her grandmother's car. They barely made it home before curfew, and DJ felt certain that the party-hardy girls, Taylor and Eliza, got back quite a bit later than that. Although, as far as DJ knew, Mrs. Carter hadn't said a word.

Naturally, this double standard aggravated DJ. Not that it was unexpected since her grandmother clearly favored those two, but it did seem a bad omen for the year ahead. Still, DJ was determined not to complain. Because today was not only the first day of school, it was also the first day following DJ's amazing life-changing episode on the beach last night. And she didn't want to blow it by getting mad.

"School's not that far away," pointed out Rhiannon. "I don't mind walking. That's how I used to get there."

DJ had walked to school last year as well. And she wouldn't mind walking today, except that she had on a new pair of Michael Kors shoes—ones that Eliza had coaxed her to buy, telling her they would be perfect for the first day of school. Now DJ wondered if she should run upstairs and change them. Maybe she should change her whole outfit and go back to her old style of casual grunge sportswear. Although she knew that would upset her grandmother, not to mention Eliza.

"I will drive the other girls to school today," proclaimed Mrs. Carter with a loud sigh. DJ could tell that her grandmother was not pleased with this setup. Still, wasn't this her own fault for boarding this many girls? She should've considered there might be transportation problems down the line.

Eliza smiled at DJ now. "So, do you want to ride with us then?"

DJ glanced over at Casey and Rhiannon. These two still looked like the Carter House misfits, although at least Rhiannon was trying. Casey, on the other hand, could clearly not care less. DJ briefly considered abandoning them to ride with Eliza—in the cool car. And maybe she would've done just that yesterday. But today things were different. She was different. And so she simply shook her head. "No, that's okay, Eliza. I can ride with my grandmother today."

Eliza frowned. "Are you sure?"

"Yeah, but thanks anyway." DJ could tell that Eliza was not happy about her choice. And she suspected that Eliza had hoped to make a flashy entrance this morning, probably with Taylor on one side and DJ on the other—maybe with Kriti trailing slightly behind them like a handmaid. And, of course, Eliza probably hoped that Rhiannon and Casey, who did not measure up to her fastidious fashion standards, would lag somewhere far, far behind.

"Well, I'm going up to put on my finishing touches," said Eliza lightly. "And then I'll be ready." As if on cue, the breakfast table began to vacate. And before long, they were all on their way to school. The sporty white Porsche, with its three fashionable girls, drove about a block ahead, while Mrs. Carter's more sensible silver Mercedes followed discretely behind.

Rhiannon and Casey sat silently in the backseat, and DJ sat next to her grandmother, wondering what school would be like this year. Feeling nervous, she fidgeted with the handle of her Hermès bag. Of course, this only reminded her of that embarrassing moment at the beach when Taylor had used the contents in the purse to humiliate her. Still, it seemed that DJ and Conner had made it past that. It seemed that he had really liked her. And she knew she liked him. They'd even gone out since then. And after that, it seemed that their relationship had begun to unravel.

Still, she couldn't put her finger on what had gone wrong between them last night. Maybe she would never know. On one hand, she told herself that it might be for the best. After all, she had just invited Jesus into her heart. Perhaps that was what she needed to focus on for the time being. And yet, she couldn't deny that she still really liked Conner. And she still wanted him to like her. She tried to block the disturbing image of him and Taylor dancing together last night. Or Taylor's superior expression this morning. Like she'd won. And she reminded herself that Conner had kissed her — before he'd said what sounded like a final good-bye. None of it made much sense. And thinking about it just frustrated her more.

DJ suddenly remembered what Rhiannon had told her before they'd gone to bed last night. "If you're stressing about something, just pray. There's actually a verse in the Bible that says to do this."

Well, DJ wasn't sure she really knew how to pray, but she *was* definitely stressing over Conner. And for that reason, as Mrs. Carter turned down the road to the school, DJ made a feeble attempt to pray. Naturally, she did this silently. No way was she going to start praying out loud with her critical grandmother and Casey, the rebel girl, listening in. She said the words silently inside her head. She just hoped that God could hear her, and that he was listening. And, by the time Mrs. Carter pulled in front of the school, DJ felt amazingly calm. Maybe this prayer thing really did work.

"Will you pick us up afterward?" asked DJ.

Her grandmother nodded. "At three?"

"That's about right," said DJ. "Although I have volleyball after school. And Kriti said she might try out too. In that case, everyone would fit in Eliza's car."

"Wouldn't that be delightful?!" Mrs. Carter seemed relieved now, and DJ suspected she was calculating how much afternoon naptime she was willing to sacrifice for the sake of the girls. "How about if you give me a call when you know for sure, Desiree?"

"Okay."

Mrs. Carter smiled and waved. "Have a nice day, girls."

Rhiannon politely thanked her, and DJ grabbed her gym bag and waved, but Casey just grunted as if this prospect of having a good day was highly unlikely.

Unfortunately, that would probably be the case with Casey. Going to Crescent Cove High dressed like Goth Girl meets Punk Rocker might not go over too well. Just this morning, DJ had tried to warn Casey of this, but the stubborn girl was not ready to listen to anyone. Still, it seemed a little unfair that DJ and Rhiannon were stuck walking into the building with Casey. It was her choice to stand out like a loser, but why did she have to subject them to it as well? Then, when DJ imagined what the three of them must look like together, she almost laughed. Almost. She just hoped, as they headed for the school's entrance, that others would have as much self-control. What a whacky threesome.

DJ, thanks to her grandmother's and Eliza's fashion intervention, looked fairly stylish. Although, according to Casey, DJ had simply been transformed into "an Eliza clone." Casey, in total contrast, with her safety-pin-pierced brows and skull T-shirt and black lace-up boots, looked freaky weird. This was aside from the fact that her hair—cut in a short Mohawk and dyed jet black with an electric-blue stripe down the middle—was a real show stopper. Then there was Rhiannon, who DJ thought actually looked sort of cool in her own unique design of "recycled" retro clothes and funky-junky jewelry. Unfortunately this was also a style that some of the snobby mean girls would be glad to take turns slamming. Yes, they were making quite an entrance.

"Hey, DJ," called Eliza from behind them.

DJ paused at the top of the steps and then turned to see Eliza, Taylor, and Kriti crossing the street from the student parking lot and casually strolling toward them. DJ waved and waited, but Casey just kept on walking into the school as if she was resolved to get this over with ASAP—not unlike a convicted murderer on her way to the electric chair. DJ actually called out, but Casey just kept on going, didn't even look back. Whatever.

"Here we go, girls," said Eliza with a smile. "Are we ready?"

DJ could feel them being watched as they entered the school. Even so, she held her head up high. Okay, maybe she was imitating Eliza now, but if it worked, what difference did it make? All DJ knew was that she didn't want to take the same abuse she'd suffered last spring.

"Where's the security?" asked Taylor.

"What?" said Rhiannon.

"You know, X-ray machines, gates, uniforms ... What's the deal?"

"We don't have them," said DJ.

"We're such a small town," explained Rhiannon. "I guess they don't think we need all that."

"That's one thing I won't miss," said Taylor as they continued down the hallway.

"I'm supposed to pick up my registration packet in the office," said Eliza. "Where is that?"

"Right this way," said DJ. "I have to pick up mine too."

As it turned out, they had all registered online, so they all needed to go to the office. Several of the kids from last night's party greeted the girls and, as they continued to the office, DJ began to relax a little. Maybe this wasn't going to be so bad after all. She tried not to worry about Casey, although she did feel concerned. But perhaps this was just something Casey needed to work through on her own—like a rite of passage. Not that DJ would wish that on anyone.

At the office, Mrs. Seibert, the counselor, welcomed them. Apparently she'd already heard about the Carter House girls and seemed curious as to how it was going. DJ gave her a quick summary, trying to play down the circus element of their living arrangements, and Mrs. Seibert handed them their registration packets. "We're a little short on lockers again this year. Do you girls mind doubling up?"

"Not at all," said Eliza. She turned quickly to DJ now. "Want to be locker partners?"

DJ could feel Taylor glaring at her as she nodded and muttered a meek, "Sure."

"And the rest of you?" asked Mrs. Seibert.

"I don't mind sharing," said Kriti.

"I'll share with her," offered Taylor without enthusiasm.

"I can share with Casey," said Rhiannon.

"Who's Casey?"

"Casey Atwood," offered DJ. "She's new too."

"Another Carter House girl?" asked Mrs. Seibert with raised brows.

"Yes."

Mrs. Seibert nodded. "Interesting."

"Yes," said Eliza. "It has been."

"So, do you girls need anyone besides Rhiannon to show you around the school?" asked Mrs. Seibert. "We do have some student guides."

"That's okay," said DJ. "I was actually here for a few weeks last year, so between the two of us, I think we can handle it."

"Well, I hope you'll all have a wonderful year at CCH."

"Thank you," said Eliza politely. "It seems like a very nice school."

Of course, this evoked a snide remark from Taylor. They were barely out of the office when she said something about the espresso shade of Eliza's nose. But Eliza just shrugged it off. "It never hurts to be nice, Taylor. Someday you may even figure that out for yourself."

Then Eliza sided up to DJ. "Looks like we have first period together, as well as some other classes. Want to show me around?"

"Sure."

Rhiannon fell into step with Taylor now. "I noticed we have some classes together too, Taylor. You need any directions?"

"I suppose that would be helpful," said Taylor in a bored and I'm-so-much-better-than-you tone.

"And we have our maps," said Kriti as she slipped a paper out of the folder. "I think I can find my way to the science department on my own. I have chemistry first period."

"Chemistry," said Taylor with a disgusted expression. "Why on earth would you intentionally subject yourself to *that*?"

"It's called education," said Kriti.

"It's called *boring*," said Taylor.

"Let's find our lockers first," suggested DJ.

"Like I'm going to use a locker," said Taylor with disgust.

"You mean you're going to carry everything around with you?" asked Rhiannon.

Taylor held up her oversized Burberry bag. "Why not?"

"What about when it's winter and you have coats and scarves and mittens and things?" persisted Rhiannon. "You're going to haul all that around with you too?"

Taylor seemed to consider this. "Maybe I'll look into the locker ..."

They quickly found their lockers. After several failed attempts at the combination lock, DJ finally let Eliza take a turn at opening the locker. Naturally, it opened on the first try. Eliza just laughed. "I guess I have the touch."

DJ threw her gym bag in and slammed the door shut.

"See you later," called Kriti. "I don't want to be late to chem class."

Taylor turned to Rhiannon now. "Lead me to the music department."

Rhiannon did a fake salute. "Yes, sir." And they took off.

"And the English department is this way," said DJ, pointing in the opposite direction.

"This is fun," said Eliza as they navigated through the crowded hallway.

"Fun?" echoed DJ.

"Sure ... all these new people, new challenges. Don't you think it's fun?"

DJ considered this. "Yeah, maybe. I guess I just hadn't looked at it like that before."

"Hey, there's Conner and Harry up ahead." Eliza waved and DJ cringed. She just wasn't ready for this yet. Still, there seemed no choice but to paste on a happy face and act as if all was well.

"WELCOME TO CCH," SAID HARRY as he slipped an arm around Eliza's waist, "Home of the Mighty Maroons."

"*Maroons*?" echoed Eliza. "As in the color maroon?"

"Well, it is our school color," said Harry. "But there's actually a story behind the word *maroon*."

"A story I don't have time to hear," said Conner. "Excuse me, ladies." Then he sort of nodded and dashed off.

"Conner doesn't want to be late on his first day of school," said Harry in a teasing tone. "Which way you girls heading anyway?"

"English," said DJ calmly. She was trying to act perfectly natural, as if Conner's quick departure wasn't really a rejection, as if it had nothing to do with her, and as if it hadn't hurt her feelings.

"So am I," said Harry happily.

"So what is the maroon story?" asked Eliza as the three of them continued toward the English department together.

"Well, maroon is for *marooned*, as in passengers who are dumped off a ship—apparently this used to happen with illegally gotten slaves. If the ship was being pursued by the law, the captain would dump the slaves on an island."

"And that's our mascot?" Eliza was clearly confused. "Like we're slaves who've been dumped here? Not too flattering."

"That's not the whole story. The marooned people turned out to be really feisty, and they fought for their freedom when the ship came back to get them."

"I guess that makes a little sense." Although Eliza didn't look fully convinced as they paused by room 233.

Harry grinned. "Hey, I don't make this stuff up."

Eliza patted Harry on the cheek now. "Well, you are an awfully smart boy. I think I might like to keep you around."

Then he leaned over and gave her a little peck on the forehead. "Later." And he continued on down the hall.

"English lit, I presume?" asked Eliza as DJ headed into the classroom.

DJ nodded, pointing to a couple of seats in the back.

"No." Eliza put her hand on DJ's arm to stop her. Then, pointing to a pair of seats closer to the front, she leaned over and whispered. "Back-row seats are for losers or snoozers, dear."

DJ wasn't sure that she totally agreed with Eliza's little rhyme, but she followed her anyway. Who knew, maybe Eliza really had this all figured out. And maybe there were a few tricks that DJ could learn from this rather sophisticated girl. For starters, DJ would like to ask Eliza how one is supposed to deal with certain boys—the kind who liked you one day but not the next. Especially those particularly mysterious ones like Conner. Maybe she would ask her about this later.

DJ tried to pay attention as Mrs. Devin, a teacher who looked like she should've retired in the last millennium, droned on about what their lucky class would study this semester. It sounded like a fairly boring overview of the literary works of people who had been dead and buried for centuries. DJ couldn't even remember why she'd chosen this class in the first place—probably just to knock off one of her English requirements and make sure she could still have PE for seventh period (since that always made it easier for after-school sports). But if today was any sign of what was to come, DJ probably would've been better off in the back row because she really did feel like snoozing right now.

Instead, she began to daydream about Conner. But her daydreams were more tormented than enjoyable. And because she felt seriously worried that everything was over between them, she decided to pray. It wasn't as if she thought she had God in her back pocket now, but she figured that he might be able to help her out some. At least she hoped so.

The morning continued uneventfully. In a way, that was something to be grateful for. Last spring, DJ had desperately wished for uneventful. She had longed to simply disappear into the woodwork, but instead she had seemed to stand out like she had a flashing neon sign strapped to her chest that said, "Pick on the new girl." For some reason—maybe it was due to her makeover or Eliza's friendship—that no longer seemed to be the case.

Unfortunately for Casey, the mean girls still needed a target. DJ hadn't actually witnessed this yet, but right before fourth period, Taylor gave Eliza a detailed report. "You should've seen Casey's face," she told DJ, "when those girls—the self-appointed fashion police—started tearing into her about her wardrobe choices. Talk about brutal. I wasn't sure if Casey was going to give it back to them or run. As it turned out, she just stood there and took it." Naturally, DJ felt horrible for Casey, but perhaps the most disturbing thing was how Taylor seemed to enjoy relaying this pathetic little story.

"She actually got slammed up against the lockers then," said Taylor. "Hit her head and everything."

"That's terrible," said Eliza. "I hope she reported this."

Taylor laughed. "Yeah, right. Then those girls would probably really tear into her."

"Why did they do that?" demanded DJ.

Taylor rolled her eyes dramatically. "Why do you think they did that?"

"Because they're just plain mean," said Eliza.

"And because Casey is just plain begging for it," said Taylor. "You can't dress and act like that unless you want serious trouble. And she is definitely getting it."

"Poor Casey," said Eliza. "I wish we could do an intervention."

"A fashion intervention," said Taylor as the three of them went into US History together.

They'd barely sat down when Mr. Myers began taking roll. DJ tried not to worry about Casey, but Taylor's awful story of Casey slammed up against the lockers kept replaying through her mind. Despite the abuse DJ took last year, nothing like that had ever happened to her. Aside from the fact that it must be completely humiliating to be treated like that, what if this bullying continued or got worse? What if Casey got seriously hurt? Finally, DJ took Rhiannon's advice again. Instead of worrying obsessively about Casey, DJ prayed for her. She prayed that God would do an intervention. Maybe something like what had happened to her just last night. It was hard to believe that scene on the beach had occurred less than 24 hours ago. But she was thankful for it just the same.

After history, the girls headed to the commons. "Let's put our stuff on that table," instructed Eliza as they entered the commons. "Then we can get some lunch."

"If there's lunch worth getting." Taylor flopped her bag onto a chair and scowled. "I think I'll ask Clara to pack me a lunch tomorrow."

Then the three of them went over to get in the lunch line. Eliza spotted Kriti coming into the commons and waved to her, pointing out the table they had just reserved. But just as Kriti was placing her bag on the round table, a couple of girls that DJ remembered from last year approached her. They pointed angrily at the table, and although DJ couldn't hear them, she could tell they were saying something mean.

"Look." DJ nudged Eliza then pointed toward the table. "I think those girls are giving Kriti a hard time."

"Why don't you go rescue our Indian princess," teased Taylor.

"Maybe I will," DJ shot back at her.

"I'll save your place," said Eliza.

DJ wished that Eliza had offered to accompany her instead, but she headed back to the table anyway.

"You don't look old enough to be in high school," said Madison Dormont to Kriti. This was one of the same girls who had picked on DJ last spring. "What are you, like twelve or something?"

"Maybe she's a child genius," teased the other girl, Tina Clark, another foul-mouthed mean girl.

"What's the matter?" said Madison. "No speakee English?"

"Is there a problem here?" demanded DJ from behind her.

Madison turned with narrowed eyes. Then she peered more closely as if trying to remember DJ. "Yeah, the problem is that this is *our* table."

DJ stood taller as she simply shook her head. "I don't think so."

"It is so," insisted Tina.

21

"Sorry, but it's *our* table now. My friends and I already put our stuff here." DJ pointed over to where Taylor and Eliza were waiting in line and watching rather intently. "See," she said as if speaking to very young children, "those are *my* friends and these are *our* bags and this is *our* table."

Madison and Tina both looked over at the lunch line now. Just then Eliza smiled and cupped her hand in a cute little wave and Taylor waved too, although not nearly as sweetly, and her expression was totally serious and somewhat intimidating.

"Whatever!" snapped Madison. "But just because you and your Barbie-doll friends got this table today, doesn't mean you'll get it next time."

"I guess we'll see about that," said DJ.

Then she and Kriti watched as the intruders went to save another table. DJ turned to Kriti, who still looked a little upset. "Those girls are so lame." DJ shook her head. "Why don't I stay with our things for now." Then she dug a five-dollar bill out of her purse and handed it to Kriti. "Just order me a cheeseburger and fries and a coke, okay?"

Kriti nodded with an uncertain expression.

"Eliza will give you cuts in line," promised DJ.

"Okay." Kriti went over and DJ sat down, ready to ward off any more interlopers.

Before long, Rhiannon showed up. DJ told her to leave her stuff and go get some lunch. "Did you see Casey?" she asked as Rhiannon hung the strap of her large carpet bag over the back of a chair.

"Not since third period. I have art with her."

"How did she seem then?"

Rhiannon's brow creased. "Not happy."

DJ kept an eye out for Casey, but she didn't see her anywhere in the commons. DJ wondered what she'd do if she did see her. Would she invite her to join them? And if she did, would the others get mad? Not Rhiannon, of course, but Taylor would. And Eliza might not show it, but she'd be irritated too. Maybe Casey had made some new friends by now — freaky kids who needed to make a statement to the world by making themselves look ridiculous.

Finally, Eliza, Taylor, and Kriti came back to the table, setting down their lunches and getting seated.

"I can't believe you're going to eat that." Taylor eyed DJ's cheeseburger with undisguised disgust. "Do you have any idea how many calories are in that greasy meal?"

"Fat too," warned Eliza. "You really should be more careful, DJ."

"Thanks for the nutritional counseling session," said DJ. "But don't worry, I'll burn off all the calories and more at volleyball practice after school."

"You are seriously going out for volleyball?" asked Taylor.

"Well, it's not that serious, but I am going out."

"You actually want to hang with the jock girls and go around smelling like Deep Heat and old sweat socks?"

DJ made a face at Taylor before taking a big a bite of her cheeseburger.

"Just when I thought there was hope for you." Taylor turned to Eliza now. "See, you can take the grunge outta that girl, but you can't take the girl outta the grunge."

"Volleyball is fun," insisted DJ. "And good exercise." She pointed a fry at the salads that Eliza, Taylor, and Kriti were picking at. "And if you guys went out for sports, you could indulge in some real food instead of grazing on greens all the time."

DJ looked at Kriti now. "And what about you? You mentioned that you'd think about going out?"

Kriti's brow creased. "I don't think so."

"But you're good."

She nodded. "Yes, but I'm considering something else."

"What?" demanded DJ.

Kriti looked down at her salad and mumbled, "Debate team."

"Hello, geek squad," said Taylor.

"My forensics teacher thinks I'd be good. He's already encouraging me to try out for it."

"Why wouldn't he?" said Taylor. "I'm sure it's not easy to recruit kids, even the geeks, enticing them to put on those shapeless debate team jackets and stand in front of a live audience and make total fools of themselves."

Kriti scowled at Taylor now. "I wonder what you'll be saying ten years from now, Taylor, when I am an attorney or maybe even a judge and you're serving cocktails in an airport lounge."

Taylor laughed. "Yeah, right."

Eliza lifted her hand in a big wave now, and DJ looked up in time to see Harry and Conner strolling their way. Harry was smiling, but Conner looked as if he was seeking another quick escape route. And this made DJ just plain mad. She knew it was because of her, but she didn't know why. And if Conner was this uncomfortable with her, maybe he should just get it out in the open. This whole avoidance, running away, and hiding from her business was getting beyond ridiculous. Good grief, the way Conner was acting, you'd think she had some contagious disease or cooties or something. What was wrong with the boy?

"Maybe I should just leave," she said quietly to Eliza.

Eliza turned and looked at her. "Why?"

"Because Conner obviously has a problem with me," she whispered.

Then Eliza sort of nodded. "Now that you mention it, I did notice that you two seemed to be at odds last night."

Taylor laughed loudly. "At odds? Don't you get it, Eliza? Conner just isn't into DJ anymore. Isn't that obvious?"

Naturally, Taylor made this flattering statement when the guys were close enough to overhear her. Humiliated once again by Taylor, DJ looked down at her barely touched, calorie-laden cheeseburger and fries, which suddenly looked totally unappetizing. But that might've had to do with the rock that she felt lodged in her stomach just then. So, scooping up her Hermès bag and unfinished soda, she quickly stood. "Excuse me," she said, without looking up. She didn't want to see Conner's face. Face burning, she turned and walked straight toward the door. Look who was running now.

DJ FELT even more FOOLISH after she got outside. What was wrong with her anyway? Why did she let Taylor get the best of her again and again? So what if Conner didn't like her. She didn't have to let the whole world know that she cared. DJ kept walking until she reached the girls' locker room. She had no idea why she went there. Maybe it was one of the few places in school where she'd felt comfortable last year—almost at home. Stinky sweat socks and all. She stood in front of a sink in the bathroom and just stared at herself in the mirror. Despite the lightened hair and haircut, touch of makeup and expensive clothes, DJ knew that the same girl lived underneath. The same insecurities, same fears, same worries. Despite the pretty veneer, DJ was just the same as always.

Or perhaps not exactly the same. Suddenly she remembered that she had changed last night . . . she had given her life to God. But if that was real, if that was true, why did she feel so miserable right now? Shouldn't life be going a little more smoothly? Or maybe she just needed to be patient. She took in a long deep breath, said a little prayer, and then went back out. Then just as she was walking through a breezeway that went around the west side of the gym, she heard girls' voices, loud and angry. DJ paused at the corner and just listened.

"You are such a loser," said one.

"What a total freak."

"What makes you think anyone wants you here?"

"What makes you think I care?" DJ recognized this voice—it belonged to Casey.

"You better care, loser. We can make you care."

DJ stepped around the corner in time to see three girls surrounding Casey. These weren't mean girls like Tina and Madison, the kind who try to look good, but say cruel things and simply walk away. These were the tough kind of girls who dwelled somewhere low on the high-school food chain, the kind who thought physical violence was an acceptable form of social interaction. DJ had actually wondered if Casey might've tried to fit into their group, although that didn't appear to be the case here—unless this was some kind of creepy initiation.

She quietly approached them now, wondering what she could possibly do to deter them. The thug girls' backs were to her and Casey's back was up against the wall. And, although her expression was fierce, her eyes looked frightened. And that's when DJ felt a chill of fear shoot through her as well. No way did she want to end up in a street brawl with these girls, or anyone else for that matter. Not only would it be painful, it would be extremely humiliating. It was one thing to get beat on the tennis courts, but it was something altogether different to get beat up behind the gym.

She swallowed hard and pulled out her cell phone, opened it up, and pretended to be in the midst of a conversation. "Yeah, I'm out on the west side of the gym right now," she said loudly, and the girls all turned around to see her. "It looks like my friend Casey Atwood is about to get beat up—yes, right now, even as we speak, Mrs. Seibert. There are three girls … no, I don't know their names, but hang on, I can take their photos. That should be solid evidence."

Then, as the girls stared at her with surprised expressions, she directed her phone at them and pretended to snap their pictures. Of course, she still had the cheapy phone that her stepmom had "splurged" on for her last year. Naturally, it wasn't equipped with an actual camera, but what these girls didn't know wouldn't hurt them. She put the phone back by her ear. "Yes, they're still here … no, they haven't hurt her yet, but you better send help now or this school is going to have a lawsuit on its hands."

The three girls took off, heading around the corner of the gym that led to the street, as DJ continued to have this fake conversation. When the coast seemed to be clear, she went over and grabbed Casey by the arm. "You're coming with me," she said firmly. And to her surprised relief, Casey didn't even resist. "What on earth are you trying to do?" demanded DJ when they were walking through the courtyard outside of the commons, safely away from that isolated place by the gym.

"What do you mean?"

"I mean, why are you hanging in places where you're making yourself an easy target for girls like that?"

"Having a smoke."

"Oh, Casey!" DJ sat down on a cement bench now, pulling Casey down next to her. "You are such a fool. If you really need to smoke, go out on the sidewalk in front of the school where the other smokers go. It's not like anyone cares when you're not on school grounds. And at least you won't get beat up out there since it's in plain sight of the office."

"Oh."

"I just do not understand you." DJ could hear the exasperation in her voice. She knew it was partially due to the adrenaline which was still rushing through her, but she didn't really care. Maybe Casey needed someone to yell at her just now. "You were never like this before."

Casey frowned at her. "Neither were you."

"Yes, but my changes are mostly on the surface, and they're not the kind of things that put me in harm's way. I cannot say the same about you."

Casey just shrugged. "Hey, it's my life."

"But your life affects others."

"So . . ."

"So, don't be so selfish, Casey."

Casey laughed in a cynical way. "Yeah, right. Look who's talking."

"Fine, I suppose I do seem selfish, but I'm just trying to get by."

"Me too."

"Yeah, well, you almost got beat up just now. That doesn't sound like you're getting by too well."

Casey shrugged again, and this made DJ seriously irritated.

"Well, thanks anyway," said Casey as she stood.

"Would you be a little more careful?" asked DJ as she stood. "At least go out in front of the school next time you have a nicotine fit."

"Yeah . . ." Casey's voice broke slightly now. Like maybe DJ had actually gotten through to her. In fact, she looked on the brink of tears—now that could totally unravel her tough-girl act!

Suddenly, DJ felt genuinely sorry for Casey, and she did something that she probably should've done on the day Casey had arrived in Crescent Cove; she reached out and hugged her old friend. At first it felt like Casey was pulling away ... and then she sort of gave in to it.

"I do not know what your problem is," said DJ as she continued to hug her, "but I still love you, Casey. You were like a sister to me, and I'm not willing to just let that go now. When you're ready to get real and talk, I'm ready to listen." When she finally released her from the bear hug, DJ noticed that Casey's eyes were glistening with tears.

"Yeah, right," said Casey in a gruff voice. "Thanks, DJ."

"Get a load of the lesbians," said a slightly familiar girl's voice. DJ looked over to see Tina pointing at them now. "Why don't you two dykes get a room?" she teased, making Madison and several others laugh.

"Why don't *you* get a life?" DJ tossed back in anger. As Casey slipped off, DJ noticed that some of her friends, including Conner, were also in the crowd of onlookers. Well, it just figured. Still, DJ held her head high as she turned and walked away. What difference did it really make what they thought of her anyway? Why should she even care?

Her next class was drama, which seemed appropriate, although she wondered why she'd taken it — probably because it sounded easy. Now, despite the ravenous growling in her stomach, she kept walking toward the auditorium where the drama class was supposed to meet. Too bad she hadn't had the sense to take her cheeseburger with her when she'd made her hasty exit from the cafeteria.

"Hey, wait," called a voice from behind her. She turned to see Rhiannon jogging to catch her.

"What's up?" asked DJ as they walked together.

"That's what I was wondering," said Rhiannon. "How's it going?"

"You mean you didn't witness that last little episode?"

31

"In the cafeteria?"

"No, I've managed to embarrass myself twice in one day."

"I actually meant how's it going *on the inside*?" clarified Rhiannon.

"You mean the God thing?" DJ shrugged. "Okay, I guess."

"I mean *you*, DJ, how are *you* doing?"

"I've had better days."

"Sorry."

"But then I suppose I've had worse ones too." She forced a smile for Rhiannon's sake. "So, you didn't catch that little scene with Casey and me in the courtyard just now?"

"No, what happened?"

So DJ gave her the condensed version. "I probably would've been more cautious if I'd known I had an audience." She shook her head. "But then again, maybe that was for the best. Maybe it helps Casey to see that I really do care about her . . . no matter who's looking."

"That's totally cool that you connected with her like that, DJ. Casey really needs to be loved."

Then DJ told her about Casey's near-mugging incident.

"Wow, you're having a busy day."

DJ kind of laughed. "Yeah, if the first day is any indicator of how my year's going to go, maybe I should quit while I'm ahead."

Rhiannon pulled an apple out of her bag and handed it to her. "I noticed you didn't eat your lunch. Want this?"

"Thanks." DJ took a bite of the apple. "Are you going to drama?"

"Yeah. You too?"

DJ nodded as she munched. "I hope it's not a mistake."

"No way," said Rhiannon. "Drama is cool. And Mr. Harper is a fantastic teacher. He's funny and smart and really good-looking too. You'll be glad you're taking it. Eliza and Taylor are in the class too."

"Really?" DJ felt disappointment sink in. Eliza was okay, but she'd had enough of Taylor for one day.

"Yeah, we were just comparing schedules at lunch."

"It figures." said DJ.

"Taylor?"

"I think she's seriously got it out for me." DJ sighed. "And if it's about Conner, I don't see why she doesn't just give it a break. It's plain to see he's not interested in me. For all I care, she can have him."

"I don't think he's interested in Taylor either."

"Whatever."

"I just think she's one of those girls who always wants what someone else has. If it makes you feel better, she's even been flirting with Bradford."

"With Bradford?" DJ stopped walking and turned to stare at Rhiannon. "Are you serious?"

"Oh, yeah ... even Bradford noticed it. She was all over him during art this morning. I'm sure she'll be thrilled to find out he's got drama with us as well."

"Sheesh, why doesn't she just try to get all the guys? Maybe she's going after Harry too."

Rhiannon laughed. "I think Taylor is a little more cautious when it comes to Eliza's territory."

"And just why is that?" demanded DJ.

"I think she's afraid of Eliza."

"Afraid? Of Eliza?" DJ frowned. "That just does not compute."

"It does on some levels," said Rhiannon.

DJ still didn't get it. Eliza might have her faults, but for the most part she was pretty nice. Why would anyone be afraid of her? Especially someone like Taylor. It made no sense. But then, DJ figured, she had a lot to learn about a lot of things. She took a last bite of the apple and tossed it into the trash can by the door to the auditorium.

Rhiannon's take on Mr. Harper was pretty accurate. DJ decided she liked him and that he was funny. Maybe drama wouldn't be too bad after all. Plus he had this easygoing way of making kids feel comfortable. And before class was over, he had several of them up on the stage in a sort of spontaneous audition. Not DJ, of course. She wasn't ready to humiliate herself in public again. Twice in one day was plenty. But both Taylor and Eliza willingly complied, winning instant approval from both Mr. Harper and the class. And, although DJ would never admit it to anyone, Taylor was an excellent actress—just the way she took center stage with complete confidence, standing tall as she recited the lines in a totally natural-sounding way, tossing in a little tilt of her chin or a hand movement at just the right moment, like she'd been doing this kind of thing all her life. Was there anything that girl could not do? Well, other than being nice—that did not seem to come naturally to her. Even Bradford did a mini audition, and to everyone's surprise he stole the show. The whole class erupted in loud applause.

"This is going to be a fun class," said Eliza as they sat in the auditorium seats and waited for the next "audition."

"It seems like it," said DJ. She wanted to add, "especially if Taylor continues to keep her distance from me." At the moment, Taylor was still on the stage, standing off to the side, right next to Mr. Harper. She was probably schmoozing and setting herself up for the lead in the next production, which was aggravating, but way better than hooking her claws into DJ again.

"So, what exactly is up between you and Conner?" Eliza asked quietly.

"Nothing." DJ slumped down in her chair, crossing her arms tightly across her chest.

"I thought you liked him."

"I did."

"And he obviously liked you."

"It seemed like it." DJ watched as Taylor actually seemed to flirt with Mr. Harper. What was up with this girl anyway?

"So, what happened? Did you guys have a fight?"

"I don't know what happened."

"Maybe I should ask Harry what's up. He and Conner probably talk about this kind of thing."

"No," said DJ firmly. "Please, don't, Eliza. Let's just let it go, okay? I don't think Conner and I were meant to be." But even as she said this, she felt sad and slightly defeated.

"Okay."

The afternoon progressed. DJ was relieved when it was time for her final and favorite class. She grabbed her gym bag from her locker and hurried down to the gymnasium complex. She knew from her schedule that she had Mrs. Pandretti for PE this year, and this was a great improvement from Ms. Jones from last spring. Some of the big-mouths, like Tina and Madison, had insinuated that Ms. Jones was a lesbian. Maybe it was true or maybe it was just mean, but it had made DJ feel uncomfortable when Ms. Jones gave her extra attention or compliments for her skills on both the soccer and softball field. It had also resulted in more teasing and being called "Jonesie's girlfriend." It would be a relief not to be subjected to that again.

As fate would have it, DJ's relief was cut short when she discovered that Taylor was also in seventh-period PE. It just figured.

DJ tried to pretend she hadn't seen Taylor, as she went over to a corner to dress down. It wasn't that she didn't want anyone to watch her undressing—since she'd done sports for years, she was totally used to all that. It was simply to avoid Taylor.

"Why are you over here by yourself?" asked Taylor as she joined her.

"It's quieter over here," mumbled DJ as she pulled on her old soccer shorts.

"Mind if I join you?"

DJ shrugged. "Whatever."

Taylor set her oversized Burberry bag on the bench and dug through it until she pulled out a neatly rolled pale blue parcel, about the size of a loaf of bread. DJ tried to appear like she wasn't looking, but she was curious. Then Taylor unrolled this little package to reveal a pale blue pair of micro-fiber shorts and matching tank wrapped around a pair of rather delicate-looking sports shoes with ankle socks tucked inside. Okay, maybe Taylor knew how to pack, but her taste in athletic wear was suspect.

"Those shoes don't look very substantial," said DJ as she pulled on her T-shirt.

"Looks can be deceiving," said Taylor as she unbuttoned her top.

"Yeah," said DJ, trying not to stare at Taylor's lacy bra that was literally overflowing with what DJ felt certain must be silicone implants. Like how was it possible that someone that skinny could be built like that? "I know."

"You don't like me, do you?" said Taylor as she pulled the tank over her head.

"You're not wearing a sports bra?" asked DJ in sincere alarm.

Taylor laughed in a cynical way as she smoothed the sleek tank top down around her slim midriff. "Don't worry, I'm fine."

DJ nodded and then focused her attention on tying her shoes. *Whatever.* Why should she care if Taylor didn't?

"You don't, do you?" said Taylor.

"Don't what?" DJ looked up now. "Wear a sports bra? Sure, I do. I may not be as big on top as you are, but just the same I don't like the girls bouncing all over the place."

Taylor laughed in a way that actually sounded slightly sincere. "That's not what I meant."

DJ frowned. "What did you mean?"

"I mean, you don't like me, *do you?*"

DJ put her clothes and things into her basket now, shoved it back into the rack and closed the lock with a loud snap. "It's hard to like someone who's always attacking you," said DJ as she stood and faced her.

"Attacking you?" Taylor looked truly offended now.

DJ scowled. "Like you don't know what you do."

"I've never attacked you, DJ."

"No," said DJ with sarcasm. "I suppose not . . ."

"I'll admit that I've jerked your chain a little," Taylor said as she slipped on her shoes and closed the Velcro straps. "But that's just because you're fun to mess with."

"Well, maybe I don't like being messed with." DJ put her hands on her hips and glared at her. "Maybe I don't like being humiliated in front of my friends."

"For someone who doesn't like being humiliated, you seem to bring a fair amount of it on yourself. For instance the little love scene between you and Casey out in the courtyard today. Like what was up with that anyway?"

Okay, DJ really wanted to let her have it. She wanted to say something sarcastic and mean back, something hurtful and rude, but instead she paused and considered her response. And for a change she decided simply to speak the truth.

"I'll tell you what was up with that, Taylor. Casey and I have been friends since we were babies. Casey's mom was my mom's best friend. Casey is like family. And right now Casey is hurting. I don't know what's happened or why she's so different now, but I do know I haven't been very kind to her. I decided it was time to change that."

Taylor blinked. "Oh."

"If some people want to make that into something that it's not, it just shows how ignorant they are. I guess I'd hope that you're not one of them."

Taylor actually smiled now. But DJ couldn't tell if it was sincere or one of those I'm-gonna-get-you-when-you-least-expect-it smiles. Perhaps it made no difference. Maybe what mattered most was that DJ had stood up to her, and she'd done it without resorting to meanness.

4

STEALING Bradford

"GOOD Game," said Taylor. Then she reached over to give DJ a high five. DJ tried not to look too stunned as Taylor slapped her palm. They were walking back to the gym after an energetic soccer match that Mrs. Pandretti had called an icebreaker. As usual, Taylor had shone. But now that they were finished, she didn't even look sweaty. How was that even possible?

"I guess I shouldn't be surprised that you're good in soccer," admitted DJ. "So far I haven't seen anything you're not good at." *Well, except for being nice,* she thought, but had the good sense not to say out loud.

"Well, thanks," said Taylor. "I take that as high praise coming from you."

DJ frowned. "What does that mean?"

"It means you're a pretty good athlete yourself."

Okay, had DJ just been zapped into the Twilight Zone? Had Taylor really given her a compliment? Or was this actually some kind of setup? "Thanks," muttered DJ, preparing herself for Taylor to jerk the rug out from under her.

"I know I give you a bad time about smelling like sweat socks and all that, but I used to do sports too."

"Really?" DJ turned to study Taylor more closely as they walked. Was this girl up to something?

"Yeah, but then I sort of outgrew sports . . . or maybe I just grew into boys."

"I don't see why you can't enjoy both," said DJ.

Taylor shrugged as she removed the barrette that had been keeping her mane of dark curly hair back, giving her head a shake and fluffing her hair with her fingers so that it looked almost perfect. "Maybe some girls can." Okay, there was definitely a jab in that statement, even if it was a small one.

"Well, I wouldn't ever give up something that I loved doing just for a guy," said DJ with heartfelt conviction.

"Neither would I," said Taylor. "But I suppose that I just don't love sports as much as you do."

"What do you love?" asked DJ as they entered the locker room.

Taylor laughed. "Wouldn't you like to know."

Well, maybe it was only baby steps, but DJ thought perhaps she'd made some kind of headway with this strange girl. At least she hadn't been publicly humiliated again. Even so, DJ knew she needed to keep watching her backside when it came to Taylor. She might be acting civilized right now, but there was still a wild animal beneath that perfect veneer. And those claws were sharp.

"Why aren't you getting dressed?" asked Taylor as DJ sat on the bench mulling these things over.

"Volleyball," said DJ.

Taylor rolled her eyes. "Oh yes, I almost forgot."

"I bet you're good at that too," said DJ.

Taylor gave her a look that was noncommittal, but DJ sensed the confidence beneath it.

"Oh, crap," said DJ, slapping her forehead.

"What?" asked Taylor as she buttoned her shirt.

"I forgot to call my grandma about a ride." DJ went to her locker for her phone.

"Isn't she picking you guys up?"

DJ shrugged. "I hope so . . . I mean for Casey and Rhiannon's sake. But I'll be staying late anyway so it doesn't affect me much."

"How will you get home?"

"My feet, I guess."

"Right . . ." Taylor's tone contained a smidgeon of disgust. "Doesn't it embarrass you to walk home from school?"

DJ shook her head as she dialed her grandmother's number. "Not as much as certain other things embarrass me." She gave Taylor an accusing look as she listened to the phone ringing. But Taylor returned that look with one of innocence. *Yeah, whatever,* thought DJ.

"Carter House," said Inez. Then DJ asked about Mrs. Carter and was informed that her grandmother was napping, which could mean anything from sneaking a martini to watching soaps.

"But Rhiannon and Casey need a ride home," she complained.

"Sorry, looks like they'll need to walk."

"Fine." DJ closed her phone and turned to Taylor. "If you see Rhiannon or Casey, will you let them know they'll need to walk home?"

"Sure," said Taylor lightly. "*If* I see them."

DJ could tell this *if* meant that she wouldn't try to see them. Probably she would try to avoid them. DJ wouldn't be surprised.

"See ya back at the ranch," said Taylor as she slung the strap of her bag over her shoulder. DJ just stared at her now. "What's the matter?" asked Taylor with concern.

"Nothing."

"Seriously, do I have something in my teeth?" Taylor whipped open her bag and removed her compact, opened it up, and examined her reflection then shrugged. "Everything seems perfectly fine to me."

"Yeah," said DJ. "That's just what I was thinking too. I don't know how you do it."

Taylor smiled now. Okay, it was a catty little smile, but a smile nonetheless. "Practice, DJ. It just takes practice." Then she snapped her compact closed, dropped it into her bag, and clicked away in her Kate Spade sandals. DJ only knew the designer name because she'd overheard another girl complimenting them, and Taylor had mentioned the name. Rather, dropped the name. It seemed that was what designer labels were best for—name-dropping.

DJ didn't have her normal level of energy during volleyball practice. She figured that was partly due to lack of food, just having played soccer during PE, and stress. Yes, she'd heard that stress could sap your energy. And her day, while not a complete disaster, had been fairly stressful. It didn't help matters that the coach was Ms. Jones, the same teacher who some girls still thought was gay. Although DJ was trying to block out the crude comments she'd heard last year.

"You were really good out there, DJ," said a stocky girl named Tawnee. Practice was over and they were picking up the balls and pitching them into the carts now.

"Thanks," said DJ. "But this wasn't my best game."

"Could've fooled me," said a tall lanky girl named Crystal. She shot a ball into the cart then peered curiously at DJ. "Have you played a lot?"

"I haven't played on a team since I was a sophomore," DJ admitted. "I'm probably rusty. I'm sure I need to work on some things."

"You don't really seem like the athletic type," said Crystal as they went back to the locker room. "I guess I didn't expect much from you."

"Yeah," said Tawnee. "I thought I saw you hanging with those snooty rich girls today. I never would've guessed you did sports."

"Looks can be deceiving." DJ studied Tawnee and Crystal now, and she wasn't sure if she was seeing people through different eyes these days, or perhaps she just hadn't really been paying attention before. But their looks suggested that 1) they had even less fashion sense than she did, 2) they needed to do something about their hairstyles—both were pretty bad—and 3) they probably weren't into guys.

"So are you going to stick around all week?" asked Crystal. "Until tryouts?"

"Sure," said DJ as she grabbed her gym bag and put her clothes and shoes that she'd worn to school inside. "Why not?"

Crystal shrugged. "I don't know."

"I actually like playing sports," said DJ.

"Aren't you going to shower?" asked Tawnee.

"I'll do that when I get home," said DJ.

"Why?" asked Crystal suspiciously.

"Because I want to," said DJ. "I'm in a hurry, okay?"

"Yeah, whatever."

The truth was that DJ didn't want to put on her other clothes because she was walking home, and those Michael Kors shoes had been uncomfortable when she'd taken them off before PE. No way was she going to traipse seven blocks in them now. "See ya," she called as she hurried out of the locker room.

Of course, once she was exiting the gym, she felt uncomfortable. What if someone saw her looking like this? But fortunately, the school grounds were pretty much evacuated by now. Still, as she hurried along, hoping not to be seen, it bothered her that she was worried about this. That never would've been the case before the influence of the other Carter House girls. Before, DJ didn't give a rip. She paused on the sidewalk, switching the strap of her gym bag to the other shoulder.

"Hey, DJ," called a guy's voice from behind her.

She cringed and then turned to look. *Of course, it would be Conner!* What timing. She considered making a run for it, but then figured why not just get it, whatever it was, over with.

"Wait up," he called as he jogged over. He had a CCH duffle bag over his shoulder too. Probably just finished with soccer. But, unlike her, he looked freshly showered and neatly dressed in his regular clothes. "I thought that was you."

"How could you tell?" she asked in an edgy tone.

"Your walk."

"Oh." She started walking again.

"You going home?" He continued alongside her.

"Yeah."

"No ride?"

"Nope."

"Me either. Harry left soccer early. I think he was meeting Eliza for coffee."

"Good for him."

Conner put his hand on her arm now, stopping her from walking. "Look, DJ, I want to talk to you, but you're making it a little difficult."

She turned and gave him her best incredulous expression. "*I'm* making it difficult?"

"Yeah ... this isn't easy, you know."

"What isn't easy?"

"Saying I'm sorry."

She studied him closely. "Is that what you're doing?"

"I'm trying to ..."

"Well?" She let out an exasperated sigh.

"What? Do you want me to get on my knees and beg your forgiveness?"

She considered this. "Maybe." Of course, even as she said this, she wondered what she needed to forgive him for exactly. Oh, yeah, Taylor.

"Look, DJ, I'm sorry that I've been acting like such a jerk ... I mean since we went out the other night."

She nodded. "Yeah, you have pretty much been a jerk."

"Right, that's what I said."

"Right."

Now he just stood there, saying nothing, and looking even more uncomfortable than she felt.

"So, is that it?" she demanded.

"Well ..."

"Fine." She started walking again, quickly. She felt confused and frustrated, but she wasn't about to stand there dredging the words out of him.

He hurried to catch up with her. "No, that's not all."

"Okay?"

"I wanted to explain some things," he began.

"No one is stopping you," she said.

"Well, for starters ... I never meant for things to get so carried away that night when we went out with Harry and Eliza."

"Neither did I," she said firmly.

"Really?" His voice sounded like he didn't believe her.

She stopped walking now, turned and stared at him. "No!" she practically shouted. "Do you think that I did?"

He shrugged. "I didn't know."

She shook her fist at him now. "You did, didn't you?"

"Maybe . . ."

"You cannot be serious! You actually thought that I was the one coming onto you like that? Like I was the one crawling all over you?" She glared at him. "Oh, Conner Alberts, you are so full of yourself! I don't know what I even saw in you in the first place!" And then she actually began to run. She almost expected him to chase after her. But he didn't. And when he didn't, she wasn't sure whether she felt relieved or disappointed. Mostly she felt mad. Just plain mad.

So, that was the reason he'd given her the cold shoulder. Because he thought she was to blame for their passionate make-out session in the back of Eliza's car? Like she'd been the one to encourage it! Well, that was just too ridiculous. Maddeningly ridiculous. She was so angry that she ran all the way home, arriving at Carter House out of breath and frazzled and sweaty and a great big mess.

"What happened to you?" asked Taylor. She was sitting on the porch smoking.

DJ just growled as she stomped up the steps. "Don't ask!"

"Come on," urged Taylor. "What happened? Did you get axed from the volleyball team on the first day?"

DJ turned and glared at her. "No! And if I were you, I'd keep a safe distance."

Taylor made a face and pointed her nose in the air. "Yes, I can see why." She laughed. "But once you're cleaned up, I'd love to hear all about it."

Fat chance, thought DJ as she opened the door.

"And then I'll tell you about my little surprise . . ."

DJ turned and looked at Taylor. "What kind of surprise?"

"Go, get cleaned up, and then come down and I'll show you. I might even take you for a ride."

"A ride?" DJ frowned. "Don't tell me you have a car too?"

Taylor gave her a sly look. "Even better."

5

STEALING BRADFORD

WELL, MAYBE DJ WAS A SUCKER, but Taylor had her hooked. Now, despite her anger at Conner, she was curious. She hurried to take a shower and then put on outfit that she knew Taylor would approve, combed her damp hair into a ponytail, and put on a little lip gloss and mascara. She was glad that Casey wasn't around, since she suspected Casey would give her a bad time for "primping," although this seemed pretty minimal compared to the time that Taylor and Eliza took. She wondered where Casey was; hopefully, not getting into trouble or beat up by the thug girls.

DJ hurried downstairs to where Taylor was still sitting on the porch. "So, you are interested?" said Taylor.

DJ tried to act casual. "Maybe ..."

"Come on," said Taylor as she hopped out of the whicker chair and headed down the steps. "It's in back."

DJ followed, and just as they turned the corner back by the garage, she saw it parked off to one side. "No way!" she shouted as she stared at the lime green Vespa. "Is that really yours?"

Taylor grinned. "Yep. My daddy had it shipped to me. It was supposed to be for the first day of school, but it got here after we left."

"Do you know how to drive it?"

"Of course. My boyfriend in LA had one. He let me use it. I'd been begging my mom for one, but she kept freaking that I'd get in a wreck and kill myself. Part of the deal for coming here was that I'd get one. She made Dad buy it for me."

"Man, you are so lucky," said DJ. "I love Vespas."

"Wanna take a spin?"

"Really?"

"Sure."

"Is it okay? I mean do we need helmets?"

"Yeah, but we'll just go around the neighborhood, and I won't go too fast." Taylor was already getting on it. "Come on."

So DJ climbed on behind her. "Do you need a special license?" she asked.

"I have a driver's license," said Taylor as she started the engine. "Hang on." Then she gunned it, and DJ had to grab her to avoid flying off the back end.

"Careful!" warned DJ as Taylor took a sharp corner.

"Woo-hoo!" yelled Taylor as she shot down the street.

And, once DJ got used to it, she had to admit, it really was fun. Of course, she didn't want to admit that she was jealous—lime green jealous. Why was it that Taylor always came out on top? She wasn't even a Christian. Still, DJ pushed these thoughts away as they breezed through town like a couple of celebrities. Seriously, who would've thought that by the end of the day, DJ would be sitting behind Taylor, flashing around on a Vespa?

Then, just as Taylor was turning off Main Street, DJ heard the sound of a siren behind them. Not a long whine, but just a couple of little pops. She looked back to see a patrol car directly behind them. The cop made a gesture that was unmistakable. "Uh-oh," she said to Taylor. "I think that cop wants you to pull over."

Taylor used a bad word, and then pulled over and they both got off. "Hello, officer," said Taylor in a sweet voice. "Did I do something wrong?"

"Several things," he said.

"Oh . . ." She made a sad face. "I'm sorry. I just got this Vespa today, and I guess I wasn't being as careful as I should."

He nodded. "For starters, both you girls should be wearing helmets."

"Really?" Taylor blinked in surprise. "Well, I'm from out of state, so I don't know all your laws yet."

"License and vehicle registration, please?"

Taylor slapped her jeans' back pocket and made an alarmed face that looked so phony that DJ almost laughed. "Oh, man," she exclaimed, "I was so excited about taking my friend for a spin . . . I must've left my license at home. We live at the Carter House, and if you want I could go get it and—"

"Tell you what." He pulled out what looked like a ticket book. "You give me your name and address and I'm going to write you up a warning this time. But if you ever get stopped again—without a helmet, license, and registration—you will be getting a big citation and a nice little fine. You understand?"

"Oh, you're so kind," she said with a big smile. "You know, I always heard bad things about policemen back where I used to live, but I think Crescent Cove must have the most helpful ones in the country. It's really refreshing."

He smiled now. "Just don't let me down, little lady."

She shook her head. "No, I definitely won't." Then she gave him her name and information. DJ was relieved that she didn't try to lie to him about that. She'd seen that in a movie before, and it seemed a dumb idea.

"Now, I want you to drive your scooter nice and slow back to your house. Don't go over ten miles an hour, you hear?" Then he pointed at DJ. "And I'm going to have to ask you to walk home."

DJ frowned. "Walk?"

"That's right. Do you realize that I could be writing you up a ticket too?"

"Really?"

"Oh, yeah … it's your responsibility to have a helmet if you're riding behind someone." He tapped her on the forehead now. "And it's your head, young lady, you might want to watch out for it."

"All right," she said, nodding. "I got ya."

"Good."

"Sorry," said Taylor as she swung a long leg over the Vespa and turned it on.

"See ya," called DJ as Taylor slowly pulled away, even using her turn signal as she slowed for the corner. The policeman nodded as if he was impressed.

Then DJ started walking home—for the second time today. As if she hadn't had enough exercise! And, if she thought she'd been hungry earlier today, now she was running on fumes. Not only that, but at this rate, she would probably be late for dinner, and she didn't even have her cell phone to call her grandmother. And she could've gotten a bite in town—something full of carbs and fats—but she didn't even have her bag. If DJ didn't know better, she'd think that Taylor had planned this whole thing. Maybe she had. Maybe this was just a big setup. Taylor probably had connections with the local cops and had orchestrated that they would arrive just as—then DJ jumped as the sound of a beeping horn startled her back into reality.

"Hey, DJ," called Conner from the driver's seat of a red pickup on the other side of the street. "Need a lift?"

She frowned as she considered this. She really wanted a ride — would love a ride — with anyone but Conner Alberts.

She rolled her eyes. "Yeah, right."

"Please," he begged. "I really want to talk to you, DJ."

She looked at his old Chevy pickup and, despite herself, smiled. It was actually a really cute rig in a funky old-fashioned way, and she'd thought it was sweet that Conner and his dad had been working to restore it. Also, her feet were seriously tired now.

"Okay," she said with an air of reluctance. "Just this once." Then she checked for cars, dashed across the street, and hopped in. "The only reason I agreed to this is because I'm starving and if I'd walked home I'd be late for dinner."

"You're starving?" he said hopefully.

"Yeah, I sort of missed lunch."

"Let me take you to dinner, DJ."

She considered this. All she'd have to look forward to at Carter House would be healthy, nutritious, low-carb, low-cal, low-fat, low-taste kinds of foods. Still, having dinner with Conner ... after what he'd said to her?

"Come on," he urged. "Please, DJ, that's the least I can do, okay?"

DJ could tell that her stomach was going to win this one. "Okay, but I'm really starving, Conner. And I don't have my bag, so it has to be your treat."

"No problem."

"But I might need something like a T-bone steak," she warned.

"You can have steak and lobster if you like."

She laughed. "And I don't have my cell phone either. I'll need to call my grandmother."

He handed her his. "No excuses."

So she called, and thankfully it was Inez who answered. "Please, inform Mrs. Carter that I won't be home for dinner," she said politely.

"Will do," said Inez, like she was in a hurry. "But as soon as you get in, you better go see your grandmother, Desiree. She's been looking for you."

"Meaning?"

"Meaning, you better talk to her as soon as you get home."

"Great," said DJ in a slightly dejected tone. "Thanks, Inez." Then she closed the phone and handed it back to Conner.

"Trouble on the home front?"

"Maybe ..." She sighed and tried to think of what she'd done wrong today. Or at least what she'd done wrong that her grandmother was aware of.

"Oh." He nodded, but his expression was still curious. "So, where do you want to go? You name it, and I'll take you there."

Part of her was tempted to request an expensive restaurant—in an effort to punish him—but what she really wanted was something simple and good. "How about the Hammerhead?"

"Really?" He turned and looked at her. "You really like that place?"

"Yeah," she said with irritation. "Are you too good for it now?"

He laughed. "No, I would think that maybe you were."

"What's that supposed to mean?"

"Nothing ..." He pressed his lips tightly together and turned at the next corner, heading back toward the docks.

"Okay, I admit it," she said. "I'm really grouchy. And I'm really aggravated at you, Conner Alberts."

He nodded. "Yes, yes … it's good to vent. Go ahead."

"I can't believe what you said to me—all that crap about me being the one who, who—well, I can't even say it. But it just really ticks me off!"

"Understandably."

"And I cannot believe you thought that. That is totally absurd."

"Okay … okay …" He nodded again. "Do you want to discuss this before we eat? Or are you so ravenous that you won't be able to think straight?"

"Both."

He laughed as he pulled into the graveled parking area by the Hammerhead Café. "At least you're honest."

"At least," she mimicked as they got out.

"By the way, I'm curious … how is it that you got stranded in town with no phone and no bag?"

"Taylor."

"You're kidding."

"Nope, I'm not," she said as she sat down at the same picnic table they'd used the last time they'd been there.

"This I gotta hear."

"Can we order first?" DJ picked up the menu and scanned it.

"No problem." He waved through the window of the café to get the attention of a waitress, and she came out and asked if they knew what they wanted.

"I do," said DJ eagerly. "Fish and chips with coleslaw and a root beer float, for starters."

"You want the small portion fish and—"

"No way," said DJ. "I want the full-sized deal."

"I want the same," said Conner.

"Everything?"

"Yep." He handed her the menus and she left.

"Mr. Congeniality," teased DJ.

"No, it's what I really wanted." He smiled. "See, we still have a few things in common."

She frowned and wondered what he meant by *still?*

"Okay, I have to hear how it can possibly be Taylor's fault that you got stranded downtown." He chuckled. "I can tell this is gonna be good."

So she quickly retold the Vespa story, the joy ride, the cop stop, and how he wouldn't let her ride back without a helmet. "To be honest, I actually started to think that Taylor might've planned the whole thing as a setup." She sort of laughed as the waitress set down their floats. "But that's pretty paranoid."

"I don't know," he said as he stuck in a straw. "Taylor is a real piece of work ... and she does seem to still have it out for you."

"But that could be changing," admitted DJ. Then she told him about how Taylor had been almost friendly during PE. "Although, I was on my guard," she said. "I figured she was about to jerk the rug out from under me."

"She might be ..."

DJ frowned. "What makes you say that?"

"Well, for one thing, I don't trust her."

DJ shook her finger at him now. "Yeah, that's another thing, Conner. If you feel like that about Taylor, why were you dancing the night away with her at the beach-house party?"

"To avoid dancing with you."

DJ had no response to this.

"It's a long story ... you want to hear it or not?"

"I'm not sure ..."

"Okay, how about if I give you the condensed version?"

"Go for it." She took a long sip of her float and imagined how good those fish and chips were going to taste.

"You knew that I liked you . . . I think I made that clear. The thing is I liked you the way you *were*, DJ. I liked that you were just a regular girl, that you were into sports, and you seemed comfortable being you. And then you took me by surprise when you did that whole makeover biz. I felt like I'd been tricked—like a bait and switch."

"But I—"

"Let me finish first. So I was sort of in shock when we went out—like, who is this girl anyway? And why had DJ turned herself into an Eliza clone."

"That's what my roommate called me too."

"That night it seemed like things changed between us. You acted so formal and proper at that restaurant. It seemed like Eliza was controlling your every move . . . and then that whole parking scene—which I am taking total responsibility for now. I don't even know why I tried to blame you . . . except to say that things got out of control and that ticked me off. But I know that I had more to do with that than you." He looked at her with sincere eyes—still the color of the ocean. "Here's the truth, DJ. I'd never even kissed a girl before I kissed you. And then it seemed like you were so sophisticated and experienced and that just irked—"

"Wait a minute!" She held up her hands. "I was *not* experienced. For your information, you were the first guy I'd ever kissed. And then things started moving so fast, and I felt kind of swept away, sort of like being caught up in a tidal wave—"

"Exactly."

They just sat there looking at each other in silence. Suddenly DJ felt uncomfortable. What had she been thinking to make a confession like that? But then so had he. Still, it was awkward. Fortunately their food arrived and they could both focus on eating.

"Man, this tastes so good," said DJ.

"Oh, yeah."

After a while, it seemed safe to return to their conversation again. DJ decided to initiate it. "Okay, I still have some questions, Conner."

"Go for it."

"If you were so convinced that I wasn't who you thought I was, what made you change your mind?"

"A couple of things."

"Such as?"

"For starters, I still liked you—or the old you—and I was kind of questioning myself. Plus Harry kept telling me I was acting crazy. But then when I saw you hugging that weird-looking girl in the courtyard today—"

"That's Casey."

"Well, that just seemed like the old DJ to me. I didn't think an Eliza clone would reach out to a loser chick like that."

"She's not really a loser, she's just mixed up ... and she happens to be my roommate."

"Yeah, that's what Taylor pointed out ... that and something else that wasn't too nice."

"I can only imagine."

"But Eliza actually came to your defense."

"She did?"

"Yeah, she said that Casey was pretty unhappy, and that no one at Carter House had been able to get through to her. She thought it was nice that you were trying."

"Eliza said that?"

"She did," said Conner.

"Wow."

"Then, not long after that, I saw you with Rhiannon, and I could tell you guys were still friends, and it made me think that I really was wrong . . . that you really hadn't changed. You weren't a superficial snob. You might look like a rich witch chick, but you were still the same sweet DJ on the inside."

"So my looks are a problem?"

"No, not like that. But I suppose it was kind of intimidating. I mean the DJ I'd been into was just a regular girl. Not a high-maintenance fashion diva."

"I am not a high-mainten—"

"No, I didn't mean that you were. I only *thought* that you were. What I'm trying to say is that I was wrong, DJ. I was wrong—wrong—wrong. And I'm sorry."

She nodded as she picked up another piece of cod. "Okay, then . . ."

"Okay, then . . ." Conner repeated.

"I'm sure you didn't mistake me for a fashion diva after practice today," she said as she picked up a fry.

He laughed. "No, and that was the moment I knew I needed to win you back."

"Go figure."

6

STEALING BRADFORD

DJ FELT LIKE SHE WAS walking on air as she waved good-
bye to Conner and went into Carter House. Who would've
thought that they would get back together again? And yet, just
like that, it happened. She wondered if God had something to
do with it. Maybe she'd ask Rhiannon if that was possible. But
she was barely inside when she felt jerked back to earth. Her
grandmother stepped out of her office and, with a grim face,
pointed a finger at her.

"I need to see you, Desiree," said Mrs. Carter. "In my office,
please."

"Okay ..." She followed her grandmother into her office
and sat down. DJ had no idea what she'd done, but she braced
herself for whatever was coming.

"First of all, can you tell me why you missed dinner
tonight?"

DJ considered this. It might be easier to just make something up, but maybe it was time she started telling her grandmother the truth. Isn't that what a Christian was supposed to
do? So she told her about Taylor's Vespa, the town trip, and

being stopped by the police for not having helmets, and how she was forced to walk home.

Mrs. Carter blinked. "You cannot be serious."

"Totally. If you don't believe me, you can call the police, I'm sure it's on record. Taylor got off with just a warning, but she'll be in trouble if she does it again."

"She never said a word about this to me."

"Why would she?"

"Well, I don't know, Desiree. I suppose because I am trying to treat you girls with respect and dignity, I expect a certain measure of respect and dignity in return."

"You don't know much about teenagers, do you?"

"What?"

"I mean, I know that my mom went to boarding school in Europe when she was my age. You were busy with your work, didn't have time to be around her. Consequently, you really don't know much about real teens, do you?"

"Really, Desiree, what is there to know?"

DJ shrugged. "For starters, some teens like to act out and break the rules ... some of the teens living in this house."

Mrs. Carter waved her hand, as if to shut her down. "I did not ask you in here so that you could tell tales from school, Desiree. I do not think that's an honorable way for a young lady to behave, do you?"

"Whatever."

"*Whatever* is not a polite response, Desiree."

DJ just nodded.

"Now, you told me that you were left in town, but that does not explain why you did not make it home to dinner, or why you didn't inform me of your whereabouts."

"I called," protested DJ. "I spoke to Inez and she said she'd tell you."

Mrs. Carter's eyes looked stern, but DJ noticed that her brow was not creased. Perhaps she'd gotten her Botox freshened up today. "Inez did not tell me."

"Is that my fault?"

"So, Desiree, where were you when you were not at home for dinner? None of the girls had seen you since earlier at school. We were rather concerned."

"Taylor had seen me," said DJ. "She was the one who — "

"Yes, yes, so you say. But I wish to know where you were between the time that school let out and until now."

"I was at volleyball practice after school," said DJ in a flat tone. "I was on my way home a little before five. When I got home, Taylor met me on the porch and begged me to come down and see her Vespa. I took a quick shower and changed, then came back down and we went for a ride. It was about six when the cop stopped us. Then I was stuck in town. I didn't have my bag or a phone, plus I was starving. And Conner Alberts happened by and offered me a ride ... and when he asked if I wanted to get something to eat, I couldn't refuse."

"Aha, you admit you had no phone ... how did you manage to call home?"

"Conner let me use his phone."

"Very well." She looked unconvinced, but once again she waved her hand as if to dismiss DJ.

"Is that all?" she asked hopefully. "Can I go?"

"*May* I go." said Grandmother.

"*May* I go?" asked DJ

"Not yet."

DJ took in a long breath, willing herself to be patient with this difficult woman who was supposed to be her grandmother.

"One of the main reasons I wanted to speak to you concerns your friend Casey."

"Casey?"

She nodded. "Yes, I do not think it's going to work out for Casey to remain at Carter House."

"Did Casey tell you she wants to leave?" asked DJ.

"No. I am saying that I may have to ask her to leave. I haven't called her parents yet, but I am preparing to do this."

"Oh." DJ remembered that moment in the courtyard today, how she'd felt slightly hopeful. "Did you tell Casey yet?"

"No. I thought you might be able to help with that."

"You want me to tell Casey that you're kicking her out?"

"I am not kicking her out, Desiree. And, please, lower your voice."

"What then?"

"I think we can agree that this is not the best place for Casey."

"Because she's not fitting into your fashion mold?" DJ was angry.

"Because it appears quite obvious that Casey does not wish to be here, Desiree. The girl sulks, sasses back, and dresses like a juvenile delinquent." She cleared her throat. "That is not what I expect from a Carter House girl."

"Would you like it if she was more like Taylor?"

Mrs. Carter smiled. "Yes. That would be quite acceptable."

"Right . . ." DJ stood now. She'd had about all she could take of her grandmother for one day.

"So, you will speak to her?"

"Sure, I'll speak to her. She's my roommate. It's not like I'd ignore her."

"I mean in regard to our conversation."

"Yeah, fine . . . whatever." DJ was at the door now.

"And then we will have a meeting in the living room at eight o'clock. I informed the other girls of this."

"A meeting?"

"In regard to my expectations, the rules, and . . ." She stood now too. "Casey."

DJ left the office, firmly shutting the door behind her. What did her grandmother intend to do? Publicly humiliate Casey in front of all the girls? Not that Casey would care . . . although she might. DJ hurried up to her room. She wasn't sure whether she hoped to find Casey or not. But there she was, slumped in the window seat with her laptop.

"Where were you?" asked Casey when DJ came in.

So DJ gave her the shortened version of why she'd missed dinner.

"It figures," said Casey.

"What do you mean?"

"I mean I could tell that you and Taylor were starting to be friends."

"Friends? Where do you get that, Casey?"

"I saw you in PE."

"PE?" DJ frowned. "You don't have PE with us."

"I was skipping . . . hiding out in the girls' locker room bathrooms. When I came out, right before class ended, I saw you and Taylor yakking it up like you were best friends."

"I'll admit she was being unexpectedly nice, but I'm sure it was just so she could pull another stunt."

"Whatever . . ."

"Why were you skipping anyway?"

"Because I had journalism, but when I got to the classroom, I saw that the lowlifes who tried to beat me up were in there. So I decided not to go."

"But you can't avoid them forever."

"I can get my schedule changed so that I don't have to be in class with them. Especially not in journalism, since that's one of the few classes that I actually like."

"So you still like something?"

Casey rolled her eyes.

"Do you like being here?" DJ asked.

"What do you mean? Here in this room? Or here in this town? Or school, or what?"

"All of it."

Casey seemed to consider this. "Well, I actually like being here with you. I know you probably don't believe me since I've been acting like such a hard case, but I do like being with you."

DJ smiled. "I like being with you too. I just wish you could be happier."

"Yeah, right."

"How about Carter House and the other girls? Do you like them?"

Casey shrugged. "Not a lot."

"And this town and the school?"

"What is this? The Spanish Inquisition?"

"I'm just curious."

"Why?"

"The truth?"

"Yeah, of course."

"My grandmother, Mrs. Carter, thinks that you don't want to be here. She thinks you'd be happier somewhere else."

"Meaning, she's kicking me out?"

"She's going to call your parents."

Casey sort of laughed. "I'm here like three days and she's already kicking me out? That should impress my parents. Maybe they'll send me to boot camp after all."

"Oh no, they wouldn't do that, would they?" Casey had already told DJ a bit about boot camp, and it sounded worse than prison.

"Oh yeah. I'm pretty sure they would."

"Then can't you just try to fit in here?" begged DJ. "Would it be that hard?"

"Conform to the Barbie-doll standard?"

DJ didn't say anything. She knew that slam was meant for her.

Casey was walking toward the door now. "I need some fresh air."

"Or some smoke."

"Whatever."

DJ just sat there for a few minutes after Casey left. It seemed pretty hopeless. Really, what was someone like Casey doing here in the first place? Other than the fact that she was an old family friend. Because she really was a total misfit when it came to Mrs. Carter's expectations. DJ grabbed up her bag and pulled out her homework. Fortunately, it wasn't much. Still, she didn't want to get behind in the first week of school. Also, it was a good way to distract herself from thinking about Casey's problem. Anyway, she wasn't DJ's responsibility. DJ could barely take care of herself.

She was just finishing her geometry when she heard a knock on the door. "Come in," she called as she closed the book.

"Hey, DJ," said Rhiannon. "You better get down for that meeting."

DJ glanced at the clock to see it was a little past eight. "Yeah, right."

"How's it going?" asked Rhiannon as they went down the stairs.

"I need to talk to you about some things," said DJ.

"After the meeting."

DJ was curious as to whether Casey would be there or not. For all she knew, the girl might've hot-footed it out of here ... although DJ suspected she wouldn't leave her beloved laptop behind.

"Thank you for coming," said Mrs. Carter. "Now let's get started."

She gave a little speech that was similar to their original welcome speech, saying how she expected them to act like mature, polite, young women. How she would respect them and expected them to respect her. Yada-yada-blah-blah-blah. DJ tried not to yawn.

"And on that note, I wish to tell you that I am making you a self-governing body." She smiled at the group in a self-satisfied way. Like that was all.

DJ raised her hand now.

"Yes, Desiree?"

"Can you explain that a little more fully?"

She placed a manicured finger on her chin as if contemplating. "I want you girls to take some responsibility for the actions, attitudes, and appearances of one another. If you know that one girl is doing something inappropriate—be it coarse language, ill manners, inappropriate dress, or simply a negative pattern behavior—I expect you girls to help guide that particular girl to a higher path."

Someone snickered. DJ suspected it was Taylor, but Mrs. Carter didn't seem to notice.

"I think I have made myself clear." Mrs. Carter looked out over the group and smiled again. "Now, I leave you ladies to discuss this amongst yourselves."

"Discuss what?" asked DJ.

Her grandmother looked slightly irritated. "I believe you know what I am speaking of, Desiree. In fact, I place it upon you to introduce the topic that I presented to you earlier this evening. Thank you." Then she glided out of the room, just like she was going down a New York runway, with only the scent of her expensive Cartier perfume left behind her.

Taylor started snickering louder now.

"What is she talking about, DJ?" asked Eliza with a confused expression.

"She wants us to call the shots," offered Taylor.

"What about the rules?" asked Kriti with concern. "Do they still apply?"

"Yes," said DJ. "The rules still apply."

"This is like that book, *Lord of the Flies*," said Taylor.

"How's that?" asked DJ.

"You know, the rich kids get shipwrecked on the island and they govern themselves," she laughed wickedly, "and when they run out of food, they resort to cannibalism."

"That is so nasty," said Eliza with a look of disgust.

"Maybe we'll eat Casey," teased Taylor.

"That's enough," said DJ. She looked at Rhiannon, who was sitting on the couch with her, and wondered what she was supposed to do next. Then she remembered what Rhiannon had said about prayer. Just then, with Taylor still making crude jokes about naming Casey "Piggy" and tossing her into a barbecue pit, DJ shot up a quick prayer, begging for some help.

DJ POINTED A WARNING FINGER at Taylor. "Give it a rest, will you?"

"Well, why don't you tell us what it is your grandmother wants us to do," said Taylor. "Seems like you know something that we don't, *Desiree.*"

DJ glared at Taylor and then looked from where she was sitting over to where Casey was standing in the back of the room with her arms folded tightly across her chest and a scowl darkening her face. DJ was surprised she was even still here.

"It's about Casey, isn't it?" said Taylor suspiciously. She stood and walked over to where Casey was and just looked at her. Taylor seemed to take in Casey from head to toe, as if taking inventory of Casey's wildly colored hair, safety-pin piercings, thick black eyeliner — all which seemed to shout, *stay away from me!* "If anyone's a misfit in this house, it's got to be her."

"Give her a break," said Eliza.

"Casey," called DJ, "come and sit over here with me, will you?" She patted a space on the couch beside her. And to her surprise, Casey came over and flopped down next to her.

Once again, she folded her arms in front of her, looking down at her jeans, which she had decorated with scary-looking ink-penned drawings of dragons, skulls, and flames.

"Here's the deal," said DJ. "It's no surprise that Mrs. Carter does not approve of Casey's ... well, her distinct way of dressing."

Taylor laughed. "Like we do."

"Never mind," said DJ sharply. "But Mrs. Carter informed me earlier that Casey will have to leave if something doesn't change."

Casey turned and looked at DJ. "She said that?"

DJ nodded soberly. "I was trying to tell you, but you left."

"Mrs. Carter's throwing Casey out?" asked Rhiannon.

"That seems a bit harsh," said Eliza.

"I agree," said DJ. "I don't think she's really given Casey much of a chance. But then again, my grandmother is not the most patient woman in the world."

"And her standards are extremely high," added Kriti. "Especially when it comes to appearances."

"I guess the question is, what do we do about this?" said DJ, desperately hoping for help.

"Besides *eat* her?" teased Taylor. She held her hands like claws as she snapped her teeth like a wild animal toward Casey.

"Knock it off," snapped Eliza.

"Oh, don't be such a wet blanket," said Taylor. "Casey's a big girl. I'm just messing with her a little."

"Well, she doesn't need to be messed with," said DJ in a firm tone.

"That's right," said Rhiannon.

"No one wants to be teased," added Kriti.

Now Eliza left the club chair and came over to sit on the oversized coffee table directly across from Casey. She reached over and put one perfectly manicured hand on Casey's knee, right beside the drawing of a creepy spider that was next to a torn spot. "Casey," she said in her gentle southern voice. "Do you want us to help you? Or would you rather we just left ya'll alone?"

Casey looked up with tears in her eyes. "I—I don't know …"

"Because we all like you. If you wanted our help, we'd all be more'n happy to give it, wouldn't we, girls?"

Everyone except Taylor nodded and agreed.

Casey pressed her lips together and looked at them as if she was unsure. DJ thought she probably didn't trust them. For that matter, why should she?

"Think about it, Casey," urged DJ. "If you leave Carter House, you said yourself that your parents will send you to boot camp for sure."

"*Boot camp?*" said Taylor with surprise. "Are you serious?"

Casey nodded without looking up.

"Wow!" Taylor sat down on the coffee table next to Eliza now. She just shook her head. "That's tough. I had a friend who went to boot camp once."

"And?" DJ looked at Taylor, waiting for the rest of the story and hoping that it wasn't just a setup so that she could make another bad joke at Casey's expense. Like maybe she was about to say the girl went to boot camp and came back as a boy. Something off color and tacky.

"And …" Taylor sighed. "She never came back."

"What do you mean?" demanded Eliza.

Taylor sort of shrugged now. And for the first time since DJ had known this overly confident and self-centered girl, she seemed somewhat uncomfortable. "I mean, *she died there.*"

"No way," said DJ.

Taylor nodded. "I swear, it's true. Her name was Andrea Sinclair. The boot camp was in the Sierra Madres. Andrea had gotten into trouble. Not anything real serious, but her parents overreacted. She was only fourteen. It was about three years ago. I'm sure you can find the story on the Internet if you look. Her parents actually sued the boot camp, but I think the place is still operating, except that it's under a different name now."

"You're serious?" said DJ.

"I saw an exposé on one of those news shows about a year ago," said Kriti. "It was about something exactly like that. They made a boy hike all day in the hot sun without water. He had a stroke and died."

"I'm sure not all boot camps are that bad," said DJ, glancing at Casey who now had tears streaming down her cheeks. "Casey's parents wouldn't send her to a place like that."

"Andrea's parents wouldn't either," said Taylor defensively. "They just didn't know what it was really like."

Rhiannon was on the other side of Casey, and she slipped an arm around Casey's shoulders and gently pulled her to her. "Casey, please, let us help you. We want to help you."

"Yes," urged Eliza. "You're really a pretty girl underneath that tough chick disguise. Why are you so afraid to show it?"

"I know why," said Taylor.

They all, even Casey, looked up at her.

"She's been hurt," Taylor said lightly. "Same old story. Girl gets hurt and puts on a tough act to protect herself. No big deal." She leaned down now, putting her face just inches from Casey's. "Right?" Casey nodded.

"Well, everyone gets hurt, Casey. It's just part of life and growing up."

"I hate to admit it," said DJ. "But Taylor's right."

"But, Casey," said Eliza. "Can't you see that you're just setting yourself up for more hurt? When you go around looking like ... well, you know, like —"

"Like Goth Girl meets Rebel Chick meets Punk Rocker," said Taylor.

"Yes, whatever." Eliza sighed in exasperation. "It's like an invitation to get picked on."

"You saw what happened today," DJ reminded her. "You were targeted just because of how you looked, right?"

Casey nodded again, wiping the tears with her hands. "But people shouldn't judge you by appearances. That's not fair."

"Life's not fair," said Taylor. "Get over it."

"So you guys are saying I have to conform myself into a cookie-cutter image — a Barbie doll wannabe — just to avoid taking a little heat."

"No," said Rhiannon firmly. "Look at me, Casey. I think I'm living proof that you don't have to do that."

Taylor snickered.

"What?" demanded DJ, staring at Taylor. "Why do you think that's so funny?"

Taylor just shrugged, but amazingly kept her mouth shut.

"Go on," DJ urged Rhiannon. "You were making a good point."

"It's *okay* to be different," continued Rhiannon. "You need to be yourself. No one is asking you to become a cookie-cutter clone."

Kriti nodded. "Rhiannon's right, Casey."

"But you guys are saying I need to change," protested Casey.

"Maybe we're asking you whether or not this costume you're wearing is really yourself?" said DJ quietly. "I mean I've known you for ... like forever. And I don't think this is who you really are."

"I don't know you very well," admitted Eliza. "But I have to agree. It seems like there's a sweet girl underneath."

She pointed to a safety pin that was pierced through Casey's eyebrow. "Well, underneath *this*."

Kriti pointed to the small diamond stud that was pierced through one of her nostrils. "Even I have a facial piercing," she said. "But I don't think it detracts from who I am."

"Yes," agreed Eliza. "I'm not generally in favor of piercing anything other than ears, but I think it gives Kriti a rather exotic charm."

"No one is telling you that you can't be you," said Rhiannon. "I mean if you look at us, we're all fairly unique and different. Kriti is very academic. DJ is into sports. Eliza is quite social. I'm into art. And Taylor ..." She peered curiously at Taylor. "Well, she's just one of kind, isn't she?"

They all laughed, and even Casey almost cracked a smile.

"Okay," said Casey. "If I were to agree to this—this whatever it is—where would I even begin?"

"Lose the safety pins," said Taylor.

"And the skull T-shirt," added Kriti.

"And the army boots," said Eliza.

"I don't know," said Rhiannon. "I think the army boots are kind of cute ... maybe you just need something different to go with them. Have you ever tried them with a skirt?"

"Oh dear," said Eliza.

"Come on," urged Rhiannon. "She gets to be herself, right?"

"And maybe you could tone down your hair," suggested DJ. "Unless you're really into the punk-rocker thing."

Casey ran her hand over the longer strip of blue down the middle and shrugged. "It's kind of high maintenance to keep it up. My roots are already starting to show now, but at least I know how to color it myself."

"What is your natural color?" asked Eliza.

"She's a strawberry blonde," said DJ. "She had the most gorgeous hair you've ever seen. Soft natural curls. I would've gladly traded my hair for hers any day." She laughed. "Well, not her current hair. She can keep that."

"Thanks a lot," said Casey.

"Sorry." DJ held up her hands. "Just being honest."

"Well, you guys have made your point." Casey stood.

"But you could care less," said Taylor.

Casey sighed deeply. "No, that's not it ... but I need to think about it."

"Yes," said Rhiannon. "Sleep on it."

"I have homework," announced Kriti.

"I think our little meeting is adjourned," said Eliza. She turned to Taylor. "And thankfully, no one was eaten."

The girls began trickling out of the living room until only DJ and Rhiannon were left. "You wanted to talk?" said Rhiannon.

"If you don't need to do homework or anything?" asked DJ.

"I didn't have any today."

"Lucky you."

"So, what's up?" asked Rhiannon.

DJ told Rhiannon how she'd been trying to remember that she'd made a commitment to God and how she'd even prayed several times today. "But I'm just not sure if I'm doing this thing right."

Rhiannon laughed. "I don't know if there is a right way, DJ. I mean, you just do it, you know."

"That's all?"

"Well, no ... I mean you do need to read the Bible, and you should start going to church ... but I don't think it's really too complicated, but it is hard—it takes some conscious effort. Although I've only been doing this for a year myself. I'm not exactly an expert."

"I don't even have a Bible," pointed out DJ.

"Get one."

"Right."

"And you're welcome to come to church with me. And youth group too. That's on Wednesday nights at seven."

"Tomorrow."

"Right."

"Okay." Then DJ told her about what had happened with Conner, actually going into all the details of their conversation.

"Wow," said Rhiannon. "That's really cool. I've never known Conner that well, but hearing that makes me respect him a lot."

"Me too."

"He's not a Christian, is he?"

"I don't even know."

"You should ask."

DJ frowned. "Really? That seems kind of personal."

Rhiannon laughed. "So does kissing. If you guys are dating, you need to ask him, DJ."

"Is Bradford a Christian?"

Rhiannon nodded. "Yes. But he struggles with it sometimes. Like me, he wasn't raised in a Christian home. He still has questions."

"Doesn't everyone?"

"Yeah, I guess so."

"Meaning you don't?"

"I suppose I do ... but there's something inside me, DJ—something so strong and alive and burning—which I believe is God's spirit. And it keeps me going, you know."

DJ didn't really know, but she just nodded.

"So, get a Bible," said Rhiannon. "And I'll show you where to start reading it. Not at the beginning, that's for sure. I tried that and it really bogged me down."

"That was cool what happened with Casey tonight, wasn't it?" said DJ.

"Yeah ... kind of miraculous if you think about it," agreed Rhiannon.

"Like an intervention."

"Do you think she'll really change?" asked Rhiannon.

"I have no idea."

"Well, I'm really going to be praying for her."

"Me too," said DJ.

It was pretty late when they finally quit talking and went upstairs. Casey had already gone to bed, and DJ tried to tiptoe around as she got ready. Then, once she was in bed, DJ really prayed for Casey. Okay, she wasn't sure that she was doing it exactly right, but she hoped that God would understand. Mostly, she just wanted her friend to get better—so that she wouldn't have to leave Carter House and go to boot camp. DJ honestly believed, especially after tonight, that Casey belonged here.

THE NEXT MORNING, DJ WOKE UP later than usual, but at least she had the room to herself because it looked like Casey had already gotten up. DJ had just finished her shower when she noticed something strange in the bathroom trash can. It looked like blue feathers. She peered closer to see that it was hair. And there on the bathroom counter was a pair of scissors. DJ picked up the scissors and, feeling like a detective, used them to push the strange-colored hair clippings aside in the trash can to reveal what looked like a used bottle of black hair dye beneath the blue hair. And there on the bottom of the trash can were a couple of safety pins. Casey was trying!

DJ hurried to dress and was about to go downstairs when she heard Casey's voice coming from Rhiannon and Taylor's room. The door was cracked open, and DJ decided to see what was going on. "What's up?" she asked.

"Come in," called Rhiannon. "It's just me and Casey."

DJ went in and blinked in surprise when she saw Casey dressed in a striped skirt that was topped with a T-shirt and beaded denim jacket along with her army boots. "You look great," said DJ as she reached down to touch the rather interesting skirt. "Is this made out of ties?"

"That's right," said Rhiannon. "Men's ties. I made it myself."

"And she beaded and embroidered this jacket," said Casey. "She's letting me borrow these for today, and then she's going to teach me how to do some of this stuff for myself."

"Cool." DJ looked at Casey's hair which was all cut short now and all black. "I like your hair too."

"Better?"

"Way."

"And no safety pins," pointed out Rhiannon.

"Yeah, I noticed." DJ almost pointed out that Casey had lightened up on the eyeliner too, but she didn't want to make her feel too self-conscious. "You really look great, Casey. How does it feel?"

Casey shrugged as she checked herself out in the mirror. "In a way, I guess it feels more like me ... like who I really do want to be."

"Cool."

When they came to the breakfast table, DJ could tell that all eyes, including Mrs. Carter's, were on Casey.

"Looking good, Casey," said Eliza with approval.

"I like that jacket," said Kriti.

Casey explained that it was on loan. "Rhiannon did the beading and embroidery," she said again. "And she made the skirt too."

Mrs. Carter looked more closely at the clothes. "Rhiannon may have a good career ahead of her in clothing design."

Rhiannon beamed as she sat down, and DJ was certain that was the first real compliment that her grandmother had given to her.

Once again, Mrs. Carter did not seem wholly pleased to give the girls a ride to school, but when Taylor offered to use her Vespa and take one girl with her so that the others could ride with Eliza, Mrs. Carter put her foot down. "Perhaps you're not aware that we have helmet laws in Connecticut," she pointed out.

Taylor tossed DJ a look of accusation. "Yeah, I'm aware."

"Then I suggest you heed them, Taylor. Unless you'd like your scooter impounded."

The second day of school passed much more uneventfully than the first. This was a relief to DJ, and she suspected that Casey was breathing a little easier too. After volleyball practice, Conner gave her a ride home. When he pulled up in front of Carter House, she turned to him. "Can I ask you a personal question?"

He looked slightly off guard but just nodded. "Go for it."

"Are you a Christian?"

He considered this. "Yeah, I guess."

"You guess? Meaning you don't know for sure?"

"Well, I believe in God, and I go to church with my parents sometimes. Not regularly, although we used to go more when we were kids, but the church my parents went to kind of dissolved. Since then, it's been pretty random."

"How does a church dissolve?"

"The pastor sort of had a problem ..."

"What kind of problem?"

"Well, I was kind of young at the time so I didn't really get it. But, a couple years ago, I overhead my parents talking about it. It seems the pastor had an affair with one of the women in the church."

"Oh." DJ frowned. "I didn't think Christians were supposed to do things like that. Particularly pastors."

"Apparently, they're not." He grinned. "That's why he got kicked out, and then the church sort of fell apart."

"That's too bad."

"Yeah . . . it was. So, why are you asking?"

Then DJ told him about how she had become a Christian. "It's still all pretty new to me. But tonight I'm going to youth group with Rhiannon."

"At Crescent Cove Community?" he asked.

DJ blinked. "I actually have no idea."

"Well, that's where Rhiannon goes," he said.

"How do you know?"

"Because Bradford goes there too. He's invited me before."

"Have you ever gone?"

Conner shook his head. "I thought about it, but I never did."

"Want to go tonight?"

"Sure," he said without even pausing to think about it.

"Cool."

"How are you guys getting there?"

"I don't know for sure . . . probably Bradford."

"So, should I meet you there?" He frowned.

She considered this. "Why don't you swing by here a little before seven? Maybe I can ride with you, and we can just follow them there."

"It's a date."

"A date?"

"You know. It's a deal. I'll be here."

"Cool."

Then DJ went inside and looked for Rhiannon. She found her in the library doing homework. When she explained the plan about Conner picking her up, Rhiannon just nodded. "Okay."

"Is something wrong?"

"No ..."

"What?" asked DJ. She could tell that Rhiannon was troubled about something.

"Nothing, really."

"Come on," urged DJ.

Rhiannon pushed her notebook aside. "Actually, it's probably something good."

"What?"

"Taylor is coming with us tonight."

DJ blinked. "Taylor?

"Yes."

"As in Taylor Mitchell, spawn of the devil Taylor?" Even as she said this, DJ felt guilty.

"DJ," said Rhiannon in a scolding tone. "That's not very loving."

"Sorry. But it's kind of shocking."

"Yeah. Bradford invited her after school today, and she said she'd love to come."

"No way."

Rhiannon nodded. "Way."

"That is so weird."

Rhiannon smiled now. "Maybe not, DJ. Maybe God is working on her. I know that I've been praying for her — and you should too. Really, we should be happy she wants to come."

"But what if she's up to something?"

"Oh, you shouldn't be so suspicious. Really, we should be thanking God. And remember what she said last night about how her friend died at boot camp?"

"Yeah, Casey actually looked it up and it was true."

"Well, maybe that was Taylor's way of getting real with us. Maybe she really wants to change."

"I guess that's possible ..."

"With God, all things are possible."

DJ considered this. "Really?"

"Yeah, it's in the Bible. Speaking of Bibles, did you get one yet?"

DJ looked slightly sheepish. "I didn't really have time."

Rhiannon pointed to a section of the bookshelf. "Look over there."

DJ went over and found a shelf that seemed to be nothing but religious sorts of books, including several Bibles. She pulled out a moss green one and looked at it. "I never even noticed these before."

"Probably because you weren't looking for them."

DJ looked at the front of the Bible. "New International Version," she read. "What does that mean anyway?"

"That's just the way it was written. There are all kinds of different Bibles."

"But this one is okay to use?"

"Of course."

DJ opened it and was surprised to see that her mother's name — her maiden name — was written on the inscription page. "Oh my gosh!"

"What?" said Rhiannon with alarm.

"This was my mother's Bible."

"Really?" Rhiannon came over to see.

"Elizabeth Carter," DJ read. "Presented by Grandfather Carter."

"Was that Mrs. Carter's father?"

"Yes."

"1975," read Rhiannon. "How old would your mom have been then?"

DJ did the math in her head. "Sixteen."

"Wow! That's pretty cool. She was about the same age as you."

"I remember Mom told me that she spent summers here a lot. That must've been the summer before she was shipped off to boarding school in Switzerland."

"Oh, I would love to go to school in Europe."

"My mom said it was lonely."

"Oh."

"Well, this is very cool to have her Bible, Rhiannon. Thanks for spotting it for me."

"You're the one who picked that one," pointed out Rhiannon.

"Maybe it was God."

Rhiannon nodded. "Definitely." Then she wrote down some places where DJ should start reading. She showed her where the table of contents was located and explained the difference between the Old and New Testaments.

"Should I bring this with me to youth group?" asked DJ.

"For sure."

"Okay!"

At dinner, Rhiannon announced that she and DJ and Taylor would all be going to youth group at her church.

"Taylor is going to youth group?" said Eliza with a look of disbelief.

"Hey, nothing wrong with getting a little religion," said Taylor, with what DJ felt was an evil twinkle in her eye.

"Anyone else want to come?" offered Rhiannon.

"No thanks," said Eliza. "I'm meeting Harry for coffee."

Kriti just shook her head with a look that suggested that was never going to happen. DJ figured she must have her own religion. Probably Hinduism.

"How about you, Casey?" asked DJ. "Want to come?"

"Not this time," said Casey.

"Meaning you'll come next time?" asked Rhiannon hopefully.

"Meaning I'll *think* about it."

"Come on," DJ urged her. You could ride with Conner and me. It's our first time too."

Casey made a face at DJ now. "You know, too much change too quickly might not be good for a person. Don't push it, okay?"

DJ nodded. "Okay." Mostly she was just glad that Casey was almost looking normal. And although she still had jet black hair and a pierced stud in her tongue, she had not put her safety pins back in. That was a relief.

Conner and DJ followed Bradford and the girls across town to where CCC—as Rhiannon called it—was located. The church was bigger than DJ had expected, and the youth group was fairly good-sized too. When she asked Rhiannon about it, she explained that they had combined youth groups with kids from another church, a lot of them from JFK High. "They don't have a youth pastor and they go to a sister church, so they've been coming here for the time being."

DJ remembered the kids she'd played volleyball with at the beach not that long ago. They'd been from JFK too. But she didn't see any of them here. The group met in a gymnasium where a live band played fairly good music. Some of the kids here looked familiar, although DJ didn't really know many of them by name. After a time of singing, the youth pastor, Rod Michaels—a nice-looking guy with short dark hair and a goatee—welcomed them and gave a brief message. After that, they broke into small groups to pray. DJ was hugely relieved that Taylor was not in her small group. She just wasn't sure that she could pray aloud anyway, but with Taylor listening it seemed impossible. As it turned out, neither she nor Conner prayed aloud, and the other kids didn't really seem to mind. Then they had refreshments, and kids started playing Ping-Pong and pool, and even a half-court basketball game started up. But DJ was tired from volleyball and had no desire to get sweaty all over again.

"What's up with Taylor?" Conner asked her as they sipped sodas from the sidelines. He nodded over to where Taylor and Bradford had a fairly competitive-looking game of Ping-Pong going on. "Why did she want to come tonight?"

"Good question," said DJ. "Rhiannon thinks it's because God is working on her, but I'm a little skeptical. Looks more like Taylor is working on Bradford."

"That girl is a man-eater."

DJ laughed. "A man-eater? What is that supposed to mean?"

"She chews up one guy and spits him out . . . then goes on to the next one."

"So, do you know this from personal experience?" She frowned up at him.

"No . . . I mean I know she was trying to get me into her game, but I didn't let her."

"Oh, you big strong man you," teased DJ.

"Seriously, DJ. Taylor is trouble when it comes to guys. I hope Bradford doesn't fall for her tricks."

"Bradford likes Rhiannon."

"Things can change."

"No," said DJ firmly. "Bradford is a Christian. He and Rhiannon have been going together a while. They have art and other things in common. I don't think Taylor can break them up."

Conner just shook his head. "Don't bet on it."

Then, tired of the noise, Conner and DJ slipped out.

"What did you think of what the youth pastor said?" DJ asked as Conner drove them through town. "I mean the part about how God can make even the messy parts of our lives into something good?"

"Interesting . . ."

"Yeah. Kind of gives a person hope."

When they got to Carter House, they sat outside in Conner's pickup for a while, just talking. But after awhile, they saw Bradford's car pulling up behind them and Taylor and Rhiannon hopped out and went inside. Then Conner walked DJ to the door, gave her a quick hug and a kiss and said good night.

"I saw that," teased Taylor, when DJ came in.

"Saw what?"

"That little peck on the porch."

"Someone pecked the porch?"

Taylor rolled her eyes. "You know what I mean."

"You shouldn't be spying on people."

"I couldn't help myself."

"Where's Rhiannon?"

"Upstairs . . ." Taylor frowned.

"What's wrong?"

"Rhiannon's mad at me."

"Rhiannon? Mad?" DJ shook her head. "Somehow I find that hard to believe."

"It's true."

"Why?"

"She thinks I'm trying to get Bradford."

"Are you?"

Taylor just shrugged. "I can't help it if guys like me."

"Right." DJ shook her head as she went up the stairs. Conner was right. That girl was a man-eater. But why?

9

STEALING BRADFORD

AS IT turned out, Rhiannon wasn't mad at Taylor as much as she was hurt. She explained the whole thing to DJ the next day as they walked to drama together.

"I guess I'm a sucker," she admitted. "But I actually thought Taylor just wanted to go to youth group."

"But she really just wanted to put a move on Bradford," finished DJ.

"I don't want to judge her, DJ. Besides, it probably doesn't matter now anyway." Rhiannon looked the other way, like she wanted this conversation to end.

"Why not?"

Rhiannon turned and looked at DJ with tears in her eyes. "Because it seems that Bradford really is interested in Taylor."

"No!" DJ grabbed Rhiannon's arm and stopped walking. "That can't be true."

"It is." Okay, now DJ thought she heard a trace of bitterness in Rhiannon's voice. Like maybe this wasn't as okay as she was trying to make it seem.

"How do you know that for sure?"

"To start with, they were joking around a lot last night, and I tried to make myself believe he was simply being nice, making her feel welcome at youth group and all. But then I couldn't help but notice he was really looking at her, you know, in a way that gets your attention. But then I told myself that I was just imagining things." Rhiannon let out a long sigh and looked away again. DJ could tell she was fighting to hold back the tears.

"You're probably right," proclaimed DJ, "he was just being nice."

"No!" Rhiannon firmly shook her head.

"What do you mean *no?*" But even as she said this, DJ observed Taylor coming out of the courtyard toward them. So she grabbed Rhiannon by the elbow and started walking again. "Come on," she said. "We can walk and talk. First off, I want to know how you can possibly think that Bradford likes her. And then explain to me, if he does, why you and Bradford went off by yourselves during lunch."

"Because he wanted to tell me — *privately* — that we're just going to be friends from now on." Rhiannon's expression was grim.

DJ got the picture. "Oh, Rhiannon. I'm so sorry." She frowned. How could this be happening to someone as sweet and kind as Rhiannon? "What about God?" she demanded suddenly. "Have you prayed about this? Maybe he can make Bradford come back to you."

Rhiannon kind of laughed, but there was no happiness in it. "I don't think God works like that."

"But you told me — "

"It's okay." Rhiannon made a very forced smile. "Besides, do you remember what Rod said last night?"

"Rod who?"

"The youth pastor."

"Right." DJ frowned as she tried to remember.

"Were you paying attention?"

"Yeah ... but it's kind of cloudy."

"Rod talked about how God wants to use the junk in our lives to make something fresh and alive and new."

"Oh yeah, his theory was that it takes stinky manure to make things grow."

"It's not a theory, DJ. It's in the Bible ... well, sort of ... and it's a fact of life too."

"Even so, I can't help but be ticked at Bradford. That is so low on his part. And I thought he was a Christian. Shouldn't he act differently?"

"Let's drop it for now." Rhiannon looked over DJ's shoulder and waved. "Hey, Taylor," she called in a voice that sounded tight and forced, like she was going all out to be nice when she really wanted to smack that girl. Or maybe DJ was imagining things. "Going to drama?"

"Where else?" said Taylor as she joined them.

DJ couldn't believe that Rhiannon could be this civilized to Taylor of all people. And DJ was determined not to do the same—she wouldn't even give Taylor the time of day.

"What's your problem?" Taylor asked DJ as they entered the auditorium.

"What do you mean?" DJ gave her an innocent look.

"I mean why are you acting like such a grumpy girl? Did you get kicked off the volleyball team or something?"

DJ just shrugged, but didn't answer. Out of respect for Rhiannon, she was determined to keep her mouth shut. Still, she was fuming.

"Hey, girls," said Eliza as she joined them. "It's the big day."

"Big day?" asked DJ, confused.

"Mr. Harper's going to announce which play we'll be doing."

"Oh, right." Not for the first time, DJ wondered why she'd taken drama. Oh, sure it was sort of fun, but when it came to acting, DJ felt fairly certain she would make a complete fool of herself. Hopefully, she could get a backstage assignment and avoid the limelight altogether. Rhiannon had mentioned that she primarily wanted to work on sets. Maybe DJ could be her assistant.

"Okay, class," said Mr. Harper from the stage. "It's time to unveil the choice for the next CCH production, but first I'll give you some clues. For starters it's a musical."

Some of the kids, including DJ, groaned.

"Second, it's written by Rogers and Hammerstein."

"Is Harper gay?" whispered Taylor and those close enough to hear it laughed, although DJ did not. Fortunately, Mr. Harper didn't seem to hear, not that he'd care, since most kids knew he was married, and that his pretty wife, Mrs. Harper, taught English.

"Third, it's a war story." He paused and looked out over the class now. "Any guesses?"

"*White Christmas*?" shouted a girl.

"No, but that's a good guess … although *White Christmas* was an Irving Berlin production."

"Sure he's not gay?" said Taylor a bit more loudly, followed by more laughter.

"No, he's *not* gay," said Mr. Harper. "Did you have a guess, Miss Mitchell?"

"Did Mitzi Gaynor star in it?"

He looked surprised and then nodded. "Care to wager a guess?"

"That's okay. I don't want to spoil your surprise."

"Okay, my fourth clue is that it's set in an exotic location."
Now he pantomimed a drummer as someone behind the
scenes played the audio for a drum roll. "We will be perform-
ing *South Pacific!*"

Some of the kids cheered, some clapped, but most of them
seemed unfamiliar with the choice. Taylor feigned a yawn.
What an actress.

"Okay," he said, pointing toward the movie screen, which
was already in place. "Let's roll some film."

The movie was actually sort of interesting once they got
into it, but DJ wasn't too sure about all that singing and dancing. She, for one, couldn't carry a tune in a wheelbarrow. Then,
when the movie stopped in the middle of an exciting scene,
everyone moaned and complained.

"Sorry," said Mr. Harper as the house lights came back on.
"*South Pacific* will be continued tomorrow—in a theater near
you."

"Or tonight," said Eliza as they exited the auditorium. "I
plan to rent that movie after school. You guys in?"

"Sure," said Rhiannon. "I've never seen it before."

"I have," said Taylor in her bored voice. "Cable gets
killed."

"*Shut up!*" said DJ. And she didn't mean the "get out of
town" shut up, but more like the "shut your mouth," shut up.
Fortunately, Taylor didn't perceive it that way.

"Really, he does."

"Ignore her," Eliza instructed them. "She's probably just
making that up anyway."

"Hey, I can give details," said Taylor. "Lieutenant Cable goes
out to—"

"Don't spoil it for everyone," said Rhiannon sharply.

"Fine." Taylor walked off like she was in a huff.

"Do you think I *actually* offended her?" asked Rhiannon with surprise.

"I don't think that's even possible," said DJ. "See ya later." Then she headed off to her next class. She was trying not to hate Taylor, since she was pretty sure that Christians were not supposed to hate people. But in the case of Taylor Mitchell, she thought perhaps there could be exceptions.

By the time seventh period rolled around, DJ was extremely angry at Taylor for stealing Bradford from Rhiannon. Maybe even more angry than she'd been when Taylor had put the move on Conner. As a result, she totally ignored Taylor throughout PE. This was even easier to do now that Casey had changed her schedule so that she had PE with DJ.

"Did you hear what Taylor did?" she said quietly to Casey as they walked back to the locker room after a hard workout.

"I've noticed that you've been freezing her out," said Casey. "What's up?"

So DJ told her how Taylor had stabbed Rhiannon in the back.

"What's new about that?"

"Nothing, it just really ticks me off. I mean, Rhiannon has been so good to Taylor. She invited her to go with them last night. Even when Taylor stepped over the line, Rhiannon didn't get mad."

"Rhiannon is too good to be true."

"What do you mean by that?"

"Just that when something seems too good be to be true, it usually is."

"That's not very nice, Casey. Rhiannon has been really kind to you too. Are you saying she's not what she claims to be?"

"I'm saying I don't get her."

"Well, you know that she's a Christian."

"So?"

"So ... Christians are supposed to be good, aren't they?"

Casey laughed. "They're supposed to be, but most of them aren't."

"Maybe Rhiannon's different."

Casey just shrugged.

"Why don't you come out for volleyball?" suggested DJ, ready to change the subject.

"I don't know ..."

"You used to like it," DJ reminded her.

"Yeah, but I haven't played in a while."

"But you were good."

"I thought you said the coach was making cuts today."

"Not until after practice."

"But I haven't even been to practice once," protested Casey. "I'd probably be cut straight off the bat."

DJ glanced around to make sure no one was listening. "No," she said quietly. "You probably wouldn't. The team's not that good."

"So, you're desperate?"

DJ grinned. "Come on, Casey, it'd be fun. Just give it a try. You're already dressed down."

Taylor was coming out of the shower now. She had the towel around her like a sarong, and DJ could tell by the way she walked that she thought she was pretty hot. DJ turned her back to her.

"What's up with you two?" asked Taylor as she came over to join them.

"Not much," said Casey.

DJ didn't say anything.

"Seems pretty chilly over here," said Taylor as she began to towel dry. "Is DJ upset about something?"

DJ still didn't say a word.

"She was just trying to talk me into going out for volleyball," said Casey. And DJ wished she'd quit talking to Taylor.

"Oh, so she's still able to talk," said Taylor. "I thought maybe she'd suffered a stroke in PE; maybe she was speech impaired now. Apparently she's just manner impaired. I wonder what Mrs. Carter would say about that."

DJ glared at Taylor. "I wonder what Mrs. Carter would say about girls who stab other girls in the back?"

Taylor feigned a wounded expression now. "What are you suggesting?"

"I'm not suggesting anything. But if you want to talk about bad manners, maybe you should take a look in the mirror, Taylor."

Taylor frowned at DJ. "Really, I do not get you. I go out of my way to be nice, and you're acting like I'm your worst enemy. Why?"

"Why?" repeated DJ. "Why?"

Taylor nodded. "Yeah, why?"

"Because you stole Bradford from Rhiannon."

Taylor blinked. "I what?"

"You stole Bradford."

Now Taylor laughed. "In the first place, I haven't stolen anyone. In the second place, Bradford and I are only friends. That's all."

"That's not what I hear."

"What did you hear?" Taylor focused her attention on fastening the front clasp on her black lace bra.

"Bradford broke up with Rhiannon."

Taylor looked up. "Since when?"

"Since lunch today."

Taylor shook her head. "Hey, I didn't know about that, and I didn't have anything to do with it."

"Except that you'd been flirting with Bradford," interjected Casey.

Taylor tossed a menacing look at Casey. "Says who?"

Casey sort of shrugged. "It seems to be common knowledge."

Taylor put her face closer to Casey's now. "Have *you* ever seen me flirting with Bradford, Casey?"

Casey looked somewhat intimidated now. "I don't know …"

"Then maybe you should butt out of things that don't concern you."

Casey stood now. She looked like she was about to say something, but then she just turned and walked off toward the bathroom.

"So …" Taylor turned to DJ now. "Are you the one spreading vicious rumors about me?"

"I told Casey that you'd been flirting with Bradford last night and that he'd broken up with Rhiannon today. I'm sure anyone can put two and two together."

Taylor actually looked wounded now. "It's just not fair," she said as she pulled on her shirt.

"What?" demanded DJ.

"The way everyone accuses me of flirting. It's just the way I am. I like guys, and guys like me. That doesn't mean that I want to hook up with every single one of them."

"Just most of them."

Taylor narrowed her eyes. "You know, DJ. I've thought about all the girls at Carter House … and all the girls at this school … and I asked myself which girl I'd most like as my friend, and I thought it was you. But then you treat me like this."

DJ blinked in surprise now. "Seriously?" she asked skeptically.

"Seriously." Taylor was buttoning her skirt now.

"Why?"

"Because you're fun and—admit it or not—you're a little like me."

"I'm like you?" DJ really couldn't believe this. The weird thing was that part of her was hugely insulted and yet another part was flattered.

"Yeah."

"Care to go into more detail?"

"You like to have fun. You've usually got an attitude going on. And you're pretty."

DJ wasn't sure how to respond. "Well, thanks ... I guess."

"And just so you know, I wasn't trying to steal Bradford. I was just being myself and having a good time. Anything wrong with that?"

DJ shook her head. "I guess not ..."

Now Taylor nodded as she put the strap of her Kate Spade bag over her shoulder. "By the way," she said. "I got a couple of helmets for the Vespa. You and I should take it for a real spin this weekend."

"Sounds fun," admitted DJ.

"See ya!" Taylor waved and then walked out of the locker room like she was a rock star. In some ways, DJ supposed that she almost was.

"What just happened?" asked Casey when she returned.

"I'm not even sure."

"That girl is up to something."

DJ wondered. Part of her felt certain that Casey was right. But part of her wasn't so sure. Fortunately, she didn't need to think about it as they went to volleyball practice. Maybe that was why DJ liked sports so much. Things were almost always what they appeared to be. You played hard. The rules never changed. The best team usually won. And when you were done, you felt good about it. Not too many other things in life seemed to be like that.

"Congratulations, Casey," she said when they were back in the locker room. She gave her a high five.

"I can't believe I made the team," said Casey.

"We probably shouldn't make a big deal of it right now," said DJ in a lowered voice. Some girls had been cut today, and it didn't seem right to celebrate in front of them.

"Thanks for encouraging me to try out," said Casey. "I think it's going to be a fun season. And I like Coach Jones."

DJ literally bit her tongue to keep from saying that Coach Jones seemed to like Casey too. DJ had no intention of becoming like those other mean girls. But Coach Jones had seemed very interested in Casey. She was certainly glad that she'd come out for the team. Hopefully that was all there was to it.

"I THINK IT'S LOVELY THAT you girls are having movie night tonight," said Mrs. Carter as they were finishing dinner.

"Would you like to join us?" offered Eliza.

"Thank you, dear, but I will pass." Mrs. Carter got a somewhat dreamy expression now. "I saw *South Pacific* on Broadway back in the fifties. Mary Martin was unforgettable."

"Who's Mary Martin?" asked DJ.

"One of the most talented actresses ever to grace Broadway. She starred as the nurse in the musical, and, oh my, did she have a set of lungs."

"But she didn't want to be in the movie?" asked Eliza.

"She was probably considered too old for the role by the time the movie released." Mrs. Carter sighed. "Careers were cut shorter back in those days. Actresses and models were considered over the hill by forty." She pushed back her chair in a weary sort of way. "If you ladies will excuse me, I think I will make an early night of it."

They told her good night and then the table was quiet.

"How old is she anyway?" Taylor directed this to DJ. "Your grandmother, I mean."

DJ shrugged. "I don't really know, but I think she's in her seventies."

"Is she in good health?" persisted Taylor.

"What do you mean?" asked DJ. "Like is she about to keel over from old age? I don't think so."

"What time does the movie start?" asked Kriti.

"Seven thirty," said Eliza.

"Anyone want to sneak in treats?" asked DJ quietly, in case her grandmother was still nearby. "We could phone in pizza."

"All right," said Casey. "I already had thirds on that eggplant casserole, and I'm still starving."

"Do you girls know how many calories are in one slice of pepperoni pizza?" Eliza asked.

"No, but I'm sure you do," said DJ. Then she pointed out that she and Casey both burned off a lot of calories during volleyball practice today.

"That reminds me," said Eliza. "When is Mrs. Carter going to get the workout room up and running?"

"Workout room?" asked DJ.

"Yes. She promised to set up some equipment in the basement."

"Well, maybe you should remind her," said DJ. "So, back to pizza, looks like just Casey and I are having something delivered, right?"

"Count me in," said Taylor unexpectedly.

"Me too," said Kriti. "For one piece anyway."

"Oh, fine," said Eliza. "Just corrupt the whole lot of us. But if Mrs. Carter finds out, you take the heat, DJ."

DJ laughed. "No problem."

So it was arranged that they'd meet back in the living room in about an hour, and DJ would handle the pizza order.

Rhiannon was the first one to leave the table, and it seemed obvious that she was not feeling her usual cheerful self.

"Poor Rhiannon," said Eliza.

"What's wrong with her?" asked Kriti.

"Bradford broke up with her today," said DJ.

"Thanks to Taylor," added Eliza.

"Here we go again," said Taylor. "Blame it all on me."

"Who *should* we blame?" asked Casey.

Taylor stood now. "Whatever."

"Well, you know what they say, Taylor," said Eliza.

"Probably," said Taylor as she began to leave the room.

"What goes around comes around."

Taylor didn't respond, just kept on walking.

"I feel sorry for Rhiannon," said Kriti. "Can you imagine how it must feel to share a room with Taylor?"

DJ hadn't really considered this. But it did seem a lot to expect of anyone, even a saintly person like Rhiannon. "Maybe someone should switch."

"Not me," said Kriti.

"Or me," added Eliza.

"No way," said Casey. "I'd probably have to kill Taylor in her sleep if we were roommates."

"Maybe you should switch with Rhiannon, DJ," said Eliza. "Taylor actually seems to like you . . . well, sometimes."

"No, thank you," said DJ.

Then they went their separate ways. But DJ felt guilty as she went to her room to knock off some homework. Maybe she should offer to switch with Rhiannon. Or perhaps this whole thing would simply blow over. She hoped so.

It was nearly seven thirty when DJ phoned in the pizza order and went downstairs to see if they were ready to see the rest of *South Pacific*.

"We're trying to decide whether to start it at the beginning again," said Eliza. She had the remote and seemed to be calling the shots.

"Is someone at the door?" asked Kriti.

"Probably pizza," said DJ, although that seemed way too fast. She hurried to get to it before Inez, since she wasn't sure if she could trust the housekeeper not to inform on her. But when she reached the door, it wasn't pizza. It was Bradford, with Harry and Conner behind him.

"What are you guys doing here?" asked DJ in a less than welcoming tone.

"We're invited to a movie." Conner stepped forward with a disarming smile. "Are you sending us away?"

"No." She opened the door wider. "Of course, not. Come on in. It's just that I didn't know we were having guests." She eyed Bradford with suspicion. This had to be Taylor's doing. She'd probably assumed if Bradford came with Harry and Conner, it would be acceptable. But how was this going to make Rhiannon feel? And should DJ warn her?

"The living room is this way," she said as she led them through the foyer. "Maybe we should've ordered more pizza."

"Pizza!" Conner smacked his lips.

"Hey, guys," called out Eliza. "You're just in time."

"I'm going to phone in more pizza," said DJ. She nodded to Conner now. "Make yourself at home." Then she glanced over at Rhiannon, who looked uncomfortable, as if she'd been trapped. "Hey, Rhiannon," called DJ. "I need a hand in the kitchen, okay?"

Rhiannon looked relieved to get out of there, and DJ walked ahead and led her through the dining room into the kitchen. At least it would be private. "I'm sure this is Taylor's doing," she said. "I can't imagine what she's up to."

"It doesn't really matter," said Rhiannon sadly.

"Yes, it does," insisted DJ. "It's just plain mean."

Rhiannon took in a choppy breath. "I'm trying to be mature about this. Really, I am. But it's hard. And Taylor isn't helping much either."

"Of course, it's hard. Taylor is the most selfish person I've ever met. And I feel so bad that you're stuck rooming with her."

"It is pretty awkward."

"Look, Rhiannon. If you want to switch, I will. You can room with Casey. You guys get along okay, don't you?"

"You don't have to—"

"No," she insisted. "I think I do."

Rhiannon hugged her now. "Thank you, DJ. You really are a good friend."

"I'm trying to be a good Christian too," admitted DJ. "But sometimes, like when I get mad at Taylor, I sort of forget."

"Yeah, I have to admit that I've entertained a few fantasies myself."

DJ tried not to look shocked. "Really?"

Rhiannon looked uncomfortable. "Yes, it's kind of embarrassing to say it out loud, but I've imagined her being publicly humiliated, and I've even wished that the mean girls would get her cornered behind the gym and really let her have it."

"No way!"

Rhiannon nodded. "Yeah. I'm a Christian, but I'm not perfect."

"Well, that's kind of a relief."

"Even so, I'd like to handle this right. I've been praying for God to help me."

"Right." DJ pressed her lips together. How could she fault Rhiannon for taking her faith this seriously? Besides, DJ reminded herself, Rhiannon had a pretty easy-going sort of temperament. DJ had noticed that last year when she'd seen Rhiannon interacting with her mom. At times, DJ had wished that Rhiannon would stand up to her mom and tell the stupid woman off. But Rhiannon never had. At least not when DJ was there to witness it. Still, it seemed nothing short of saintliness that Rhiannon hadn't torn into Taylor yet. DJ felt certain she wouldn't do half as well in the same situation. And she couldn't believe she'd just offered to become Taylor's roommate. Had she lost her mind?

"In light of our unexpected visitors, I think I'll skip the movie tonight," said Rhiannon. Then she brightened slightly. "In fact, maybe I'll use the time to switch some things into your room while everyone is down there. If you don't mind?"

"Sure," said DJ, although the idea of them doing the switch tonight had not occurred to her.

"Do you want me to move anything for you while I'm at it?" she asked.

"Sure, if you want. I suppose you'll need some drawer and closet space for your things. Go ahead and do some switching if you want. Then maybe we can tackle the rest of it during the weekend."

"I'm sure Taylor will be glad to get rid of me," said Rhiannon.

"Only because she's crazy."

"Thanks again. I really appreciate it."

"I think I hear Eliza calling. I better phone in for some more pizza," she said. "Want me to make any excuses for you not being there for the movie?"

Rhiannon shook her head. "No. I doubt anyone will notice anyway."

"I'll notice."

"Thanks."

But when DJ returned to the living room, where they'd all decided to watch the movie from the beginning since half of them hadn't seen it yet, it seemed that Rhiannon was right. They didn't seem to notice that she was missing. Conner had saved DJ a space beside him, and Harry and Eliza were already in the loveseat. For some reason DJ felt relieved to see that Taylor and Bradford weren't sitting together. Of course, she figured that might change before the night was over. But at least Rhiannon wouldn't be around to witness it if it did. She wondered how Taylor would react to swapping roommates.

About thirty minutes into the movie, the pizzas arrived. DJ had asked them to hold her earlier order and deliver them both together, along with a selection of sodas. Fortunately, Eliza offered to cover the bill, and Taylor, probably just wanting attention, threw in a pretty generous tip. Conner helped DJ bring the order in, but when they got back, Taylor and Bradford had taken their spot and were now sitting together on the couch. As she set the food items on the oversized coffee table, DJ tossed Taylor a glance, which Taylor ignored. Then she and Conner made themselves comfortable on the big floor cushions.

The movie was actually pretty good in a corny, old-fashioned sort of way. One of the underlying themes had to do with prejudice, and DJ was surprised that a goofy musical made fifty years ago would contain such a strong statement.

"Don't you guys think that Taylor should play Liat?" suggested Bradford.

"You mean because she's so sweet and innocent," teased Eliza.

"No, he means because my skin is dark like hers," said Taylor.

109

"So is Bloody Mary's," said DJ. "Maybe Taylor should play her … or would that be considered typecasting?"

Taylor gave DJ a withering look. And DJ suddenly remembered she'd be sharing this girl's room tonight. "Just kidding," said DJ quickly. "Actually, Taylor does look a little bit like Liat."

"Why thank you," said Taylor.

"I think Eliza should play Nellie," said Harry fondly. "Wouldn't she be perfect?"

"That depends on whether she can sing or not," said Taylor in a slightly snooty tone. She peered at Eliza. "Can you?"

Eliza gave her a coy look then shrugged. "I guess we'll have to wait and see."

"Bradford can sing," said Harry. "Maybe he can play the Lieutenant."

Bradford grinned and slipped his arm around Taylor now. "Yeah, I'll be Joe Cable, and you can be my Polynesian baby."

"And by the end of the show, you'll be dead," she said as she stood up.

He made a sad face. "But you'll be crying for me."

"When are auditions anyway?" asked Harry.

"Next week."

"Sorry to end the party," announced DJ when she noticed the clock. "But we're supposed to vacate this room by ten on school nights."

"Not that Mrs. Carter would notice," said Taylor with a yawn. "But I'm sleepy anyway."

That seemed to break it up. Eliza and DJ saw the guys to the door, but DJ could tell that Bradford was disappointed when Taylor didn't do the same.

"Thanks for everything," said Conner as they went down into the yard for what she suspected would be a more private good night.

"Thanks for coming," said DJ.

Then he leaned down and kissed her. "See ya tomorrow."

"See ya." She stepped away from him and went back on the porch and waved. Eliza and Harry were still standing by the Jeep. Maybe Eliza planned to stay out there all night, but DJ did not. She went into the house and closed the door. She wished she'd thought to ask Conner who'd invited them here tonight, but she felt pretty certain it was Taylor's doing. Just one more subtle way to ensure that she was stealing Bradford from Rhiannon. Well, at least Rhiannon didn't have to sit down there and witness the whole thing herself. That's probably what Taylor had intended.

Then, as DJ went up the stairs, she remembered that starting tonight she was Taylor's new roommate. Oh, what had she been thinking? Of course, she'd felt sorry for Rhiannon, but surely there could be a better way. Perhaps DJ could sleep in the library. She could sneak a sleeping bag down there, tuck it behind the couch during the day and—

"DJ," Taylor was leaning over the railing on of the landing, "I hear that you're my new roomie."

DJ rolled her eyes. "Yeah, so?"

"Oh, don't get so excited," said Taylor.

"I'm only doing this for Rhiannon."

"Whatever you say." Taylor didn't seem convinced.

"I am. It seemed totally unfair for her to be stuck with you after all you've done to her."

"All I've done to her?" Taylor shook her head. "Like I'm the Wicked Witch of the West. Whatever."

Out of habit, DJ started to go into her own room.

"Oops," said Taylor. "Wrong room."

"I need to get some things."

"You sure?" asked Taylor. "Looked to me like Rhiannon got you pretty much moved."

"Maybe I just want to check and make sure," said DJ. This time she knocked first and then went in.

Rhiannon was sitting on what had been DJ's bed. And Casey was sitting across from her. It looked as if they'd been in the midst of a serious conversation. "Sorry to interrupt," she said uncomfortably. "I just wanted to see if there was anything else to move." She glanced around at what had been her old room. First hers alone ... then hers and Casey's. Already it felt different.

"I think I got it all, but feel free to look around," said Rhiannon. "Casey showed me what was yours in the bathroom. We just took the last of it over."

DJ walked around and looked, but it did seem that every trace of her had been removed from the room. "You okay with this, Casey?" she asked. "We didn't have a chance to warn you."

"Yeah, it's fine. You snore anyway, DJ."

"I do not."

"You do too. Sometimes anyway." Casey actually smiled now. "I think it was nice of you to do the switcheroo. Hopefully Taylor won't put a hex on you in your sleep."

"Yeah, thanks."

"You going to be okay?" asked Rhiannon with concern.

DJ forced a smile. "I'm fine."

"I'll be praying for you," promised Rhiannon.

"Thanks. Maybe you have a crucifix you can loan me ..."

"Huh?" Rhiannon looked confused.

DJ made a cross out of her two forefingers, as if warding off a vampire or evil spirit. "You know, to keep the devil girl at bay."

"Just scream if you need help," said Casey. "We'll rescue you."

"Thanks." Then DJ told them good night and—feeling like she was going to meet her executioner—walked into what still felt like Taylor's room.

"Ever heard of knocking?" asked Taylor, who was sitting in the window seat and just lighting up a cigarette.

"Do *you* knock before you come into your own room?" demanded DJ.

Taylor shrugged then blew out a long puff of blue smoke.

"Open a window, would you?" said DJ irately.

"Afraid of a little second-hand smoke, are we?" But at least she cranked open the window behind her.

"If you had any sense you would be too. And don't forget the rules, Taylor."

"Glad you could make it home tonight, roomie." Taylor was using a phony-sounding cheerful tone. "Although it's past curfew—not that you'd forget the rules."

DJ looked around the room and sighed. Her new home. Whoopee. She checked her side of the closet and some drawers.

"Everything in its place?"

DJ ignored Taylor as she took out her faded pajama bottoms and a tank top, her usual sleeping gear. At least Rhiannon had done a nice job of putting her things away for her. But then these rooms were outfitted fairly much the same, so she'd probably just emptied one drawer into another. Still, it was thoughtful. But then again that was Rhiannon—thoughtful.

"You're not much fun tonight," said Taylor. "Here I was all excited about my new roomie, and you're acting like your grumpy old self again."

"Look," said DJ. She was fed up with Taylor's endless teasing and game-playing. "It's not like I'm thrilled to be your roommate, Taylor. But we might as well try to make the best of it."

"Hey, that's what I've been trying to do. You're the one who keeps acting all snotty and mean to me, like you're so much better than I am. Miss Superiority Complex."

"Like you should talk."

"What exactly is your problem anyway?" demanded Taylor. She snuffed out her cigarette and then stood up, putting both hands on her hips and just staring. "It's like you're always in a snit about something or other. Don't you know how to let things go?"

"Not when I'm still ticked at you for stealing Bradford from Rhiannon."

"Here we go with that stupid stealing Bradford theory again. First of all, just how does one *steal* a boyfriend anyway? Is that even possible? You make it sound like Bradford is some helpless victim. Don't you think he has a choice in this? All I've done is be myself. I can't help it if Bradford likes me. Can't you get over it, DJ?"

"No, I can't." She shook her finger at Taylor. "Speaking of victims, tell me, Taylor, why is it okay for you to act like you're this helpless femme fatale, and you can't help that anything in pants falls head over heels in love with you."

Taylor laughed, but it was a cold, harsh laugh. "Is that what you think I do?"

"You've said as much."

"Yeah, right!"

"Okay then, what was up with you inviting Bradford to the movie? Then you don't even tell anyone. And Rhiannon is so crushed when she sees him that she can't even watch the movie. Tell me that wasn't some really tasteless, cruel joke."

"*Me?*" Taylor looked honestly indignant now. "You're accusing *me* of inviting Bradford tonight?" She really was an excellent actress, and she probably would end up getting the lead part in the musical.

"Are you saying you *didn't* invite Bradford? Or that you didn't include Harry and Conner to create a little smoke screen?"

"That's what I'm saying."

"You honestly expect me to believe it?"

"Frankly, my dear, I don't give a rip whether you believe me or not." Taylor started getting ready for bed. "I've had more than enough of you for one night, DJ. If this is any indicator of what rooming with you is going to be like, I might just beg Rhiannon to come back."

"Like she even would."

"She probably would." Taylor glared at DJ. "Because even though Rhiannon is totally naïve, at least she's nice. Unlike some people who go around falsely accusing others and acting like they're so superior."

"Taylor," demanded DJ, "who else would've invited Bradford?"

"I thought maybe you did." Taylor turned her back now, removed her shirt and her bra, and slipped on a silky pink nightshirt.

"Yeah, right."

"Maybe Rhiannon did?" Taylor still had her back to DJ as she put her clothes away.

"Get real."

"Then it had to be Eliza, because it wasn't me."

"You swear you didn't invite Bradford?"

Taylor turned around and narrowed her eyes at DJ now. "If I want to swear, I'll swear until the cows come home. But I'm not going to let you push me around, DJ. If you want to blame me, fine. I really don't give a rip." Then Taylor stomped off into the bathroom and slammed the door.

DJ knew she should just let it go, but she couldn't stand the idea of Taylor messing with people and then lying and expecting to get away with it. It just wasn't fair. There seemed one easy way to settle this. She went to Eliza's room and tapped on the door. To her surprise, it was already dark.

"Sorry," she said as she poked her head in.

Eliza turned on the bedside lamp and sat up. "It sounds like World War III out there. What is going on anyway?"

"I need to know something," DJ whispered. "Rhiannon and I switched rooms. And Taylor and I are already having a great big fight. She totally denies inviting Bradford here tonight. I know that I didn't. And Rhiannon sure didn't. And neither did Casey. I figured if I talked to you guys, I could nail her and—"

"Taylor *didn't* invite Bradford," said Eliza.

"She didn't?"

"No ... I did."

DJ frowned. "Why?"

"Oh, I had this half-baked idea of trying to get Rhiannon and Bradford back together. I talked to him after drama and told him how brokenhearted she was, and he actually seemed to care. I invited him here just so he could at least be nice to her, maybe cheer her up. And then she runs off and disappears."

"And he cozies up with Taylor."

"Yeah, it kind of backfired on me."

"Are you guys about done?" demanded Kriti in a cranky voice. "Some of us would like to get some sleep around here."

"Good night," said DJ, quietly closing the door behind her.

She stood in the hallway for a few minutes trying to wrap her head around this little dilemma. Wasn't this just perfect? Her first night rooming with Taylor and she'd falsely accused her. Did this mean she had to apologize now? That just seemed so wrong.

TAYLOR WAS STILL IN THE BATHROOM, so DJ quickly got ready for bed and considered pretending to be asleep. Instead, she prayed. It was the first time she'd actually prayed today, and she felt guilty for that. Still, she knew she needed some help just now. She remembered how Rhiannon had promised to pray for her tonight. And if DJ was going to apologize to Taylor, she'd need some divine help.

When Taylor emerged from the bathroom, DJ felt ready. "Taylor, I need to tell you something . . ."

"Wow, I can hardly wait," said Taylor as she peeled the comforter back from her bed and punched a down pillow.

"I was wrong."

Taylor turned and stared at DJ. "What?"

"I was wrong to accuse you of inviting Bradford tonight. I thought you'd devised some kind of evil scheme to sabotage Rhiannon. And I was wrong. I'm sorry."

Taylor kind of laughed. "So who invited him anyway?"

"Eliza."

"Well, remind me to thank that girl in the morning."

"Yeah . . . right."

"And I should thank you too."

"Why?" she muttered, almost afraid to hear the answer now.

"Because the more I think about it, the more I like the idea of Bradford and me as a couple. We actually have a lot in common."

"Like what?"

"We both have famous mothers, and we've been exposed to art and culture and music."

DJ refrained from rolling her eyes or yawning. After all, she was supposed to be apologizing. It might cancel it all out if she made fun of Taylor now.

"Besides, after all the grief you've given me today, I figure I must've already paid my dues, DJ. So I might as well just go for the whole enchilada. Don't you think?"

DJ had absolutely no response to this. And so without saying a word, she went into the bathroom. Although it was getting late, she took much longer than usual to get ready for bed. She even flossed. Anything to avoid going back out there where Taylor was probably planning her next strategy for attaining Bradford. Not that she needed to work too hard at it. Poor Rhiannon. With friends like DJ and Eliza—who'd tried to help but seriously messed up—that girl didn't need enemies.

When DJ finally slipped out of the bathroom, it was dark and quiet in the room. She tiptoed across the room and crawled into bed. Then, closing her eyes tightly, she prayed for the second time that day. This time, she told God she was sorry. To be honest, she wasn't completely sure what she was sorry about. She just knew that she was sorry. And she hoped that tomorrow, she'd get a fresh start. Maybe not with Taylor, but hopefully with God.

It took a few seconds for DJ to get her bearings the next morning. Something was different. What was it? This room was blue ... not yellow, and her bed was in the wrong spot. Suddenly, she remembered she'd switched rooms, which meant she had a new roommate—a roommate who was already up and literally singing in the shower. DJ wasn't surprised that Taylor had a fairly decent voice. But she was totally shocked that she seemed to be in a pretty good mood today.

DJ stretched in bed and sat up. Last night, when she and Taylor were arguing, she'd noticed that Rhiannon had placed her Bible—what used to be DJ's mom's Bible—on the bedside table. This morning she picked it up and opened it to where Rhiannon must've stuck in a bookmark. DJ guessed that the colorful bookmark, with a pretty beaded ribbon tied to it, had been made by Rhiannon. Then midway down the page was a sticky note with an arrow drawn on it. She read the verse the arrow seemed to be pointing to and then she read the following one. "You have heard that it was said, '*You shall love your neighbor* and hate your enemy.' But I say to you, love your enemies, bless those who curse you, do good to those who hate you, and pray for those who spitefully use you and persecute you." (Matthew 5:43–44).

But she didn't understand the meaning of these sentences. In fact, they not only sounded totally alien, like from another planet, but they sounded totally impossible as well. To start with, the verses said to *not only love your friends, but love your enemies too.* Now, she could almost get that. But it didn't stop there. It also said to speak kind words to someone who swears and cusses at you. And to do good to someone who hates your guts. And finally to pray for people who use and abuse you. What was up with that? Who really lived like that? DJ even doubted that angelic Rhiannon could meet this standard consistently. And yet, Rhiannon had obviously marked those sentences. Why?

Just then Taylor emerged from the steamed-up bathroom. She had on a thick white terrycloth robe, and even without makeup, she looked glamorous and beautiful as she fluffed her curly hair with a towel. But when she saw DJ with the Bible in her lap, she threw back her head and laughed. "No way," she said. "You're not turning into a Bible-thumping fanatic too?"

DJ closed the Bible and set it back on her nightstand and shrugged.

"What is this? Some kind of religious epidemic? First Rhiannon, now you? Who will be next to fall victim?"

DJ stood. "Are you done in the bathroom?"

"For now."

DJ was surprised at the mess Taylor had managed to create this morning. The area by the sinks looked as if Macy's cosmetic counter had thrown up in there. She wondered if Inez usually cleaned all this up after they went to school, or was Taylor simply being territorial, trying to make it clear that she dominated in the bathroom as she seemed to do in all things. Well, Rhiannon might've taken this, but DJ was not going to give in to Taylor's selfishness. She used her arm to swipe all of Taylor's junk over to one side, knocking bottles and things over as she crowded them around the other sink. Much better.

Then she took a quick shower, toweled off, and put on her rather shabby-looking aqua blue chenille bathrobe. It might not be as plush as Taylor's, but it had been DJ's mom's, and she was not giving it up. Then she peeked out into the room to see if Taylor was still there or not. She was. So DJ lingered in the bathroom a bit longer, taking a little more care than usual as she put on her makeup.

"Are you about done in there?" asked Taylor as she opened the door.

"Sure," said DJ lightly. "It's all yours."

Then with Taylor safely in the bathroom, DJ hurried to get dressed and then headed downstairs for breakfast. To her surprise, the other four girls were already heading out the front door, but Eliza waited.

"What's up?" DJ asked her.

Eliza glanced up the stairs. "I'm taking these guys to school today."

"A little early," pointed out DJ.

"So Rhiannon doesn't have to be around Taylor. We're stopping at Starbucks to kill some time before school."

"So I'm stuck with Taylor?"

Eliza gave her a sympathetic smile. "You seem to stand up to her better than the other girls. Do you mind?"

"I guess not."

She patted DJ on the back. "Hey, you look extra pretty this morning."

"Thanks ..." Then DJ figured this meant she needed to compliment Eliza back. "I like your shoes."

Eliza pointed a pretty red toe out. "They're Jimmys."

"Who's Jimmy?"

"Choo."

"Huh?"

"Jimmy Choo." Eliza laughed. "I can see our work with you is not done yet, DJ. See ya."

DJ had to appreciate that Eliza was trying to help Rhiannon. But she did not appreciate being partnered with Taylor. Rooming with her was bad enough, but going to school with her too? Then she remembered what she'd read in the Bible this morning about being kind to your enemies. Maybe that's what this was about. Maybe God just wanted her to be nice to Taylor. Well, she could give it a shot. At least for a day ...

or maybe just this morning. She wasn't too sure how long she could pull something this difficult off.

"Good morning, Desiree," said Mrs. Carter. "Eliza took some of the girls to school early. Apparently they had something they needed to attend to."

"Right." DJ nodded as she sat down. "Eliza told me."

"I've been thinking about something, Desiree." She set her coffee cup back in the saucer.

"Yes?" DJ waited, unsure as to whether this would be a good something or a bad something.

"We seem to be in need of another vehicle."

"Huh?"

"Ladies do not say, huh, Desiree. *Pardon me.*"

"Yeah, whatever."

Her grandmother narrowed her eyes slightly. "Well, I suppose that Rome wasn't built in a day."

"Huh?"

"Pardon me."

"What was it you were thinking?" asked DJ, desperate to move on.

"I think it's time to get you a car."

"Me?" DJ sat up a little straighter now. "A car?"

"Yes. We will go looking tomorrow morning. Please, plan on it."

"Looking for what?" asked Taylor as she came into the dining room. Then she paused and politely said good morning to Mrs. Carter.

"A car," said Mrs. Carter. "I have decided with six girls going in different directions, it would be wise to get a car for Desiree."

"Cool," said Taylor, winking at DJ.

"It isn't that I mind driving you girls to school." Mrs. Carter smiled. "But I have never seen myself as a chauffeur."

"I have my Vespa," said Taylor.

"That may be fine when the weather is nice like this, but winter in Connecticut isn't like what you're used to in southern California, Taylor."

"Yes, I suppose."

"Perhaps you would like to join Desiree and me in looking for a vehicle tomorrow morning."

"Sure," said Taylor. She looked around the table now. "Hey, where's everyone?"

So Mrs. Carter relayed Eliza's little fib, and then Taylor offered to give DJ a ride on her Vespa this morning.

"That's okay," said DJ quickly.

"You have helmets now?" asked Mrs. Carter.

"I do."

"That would be lovely," said Mrs. Carter. Then she frowned. "But you girls are wearing skirts today. That doesn't seem very ladylike ... to ride on a motor scooter like that."

"Girls do it all the time back in LA."

"Well, then ..."

"And, of course, you can be assured that both Desiree and I will be perfect ladies while riding."

Mrs. Carter smiled. "Yes, of course."

DJ was tempted to say she'd rather walk to school than be stuck with Taylor on the back of the Vespa, but then she remembered today's goal to be nice to her enemy.

"Have a good day, girls," said Mrs. Carter. "By the way, Desiree, will you let the others know that I won't be at dinner tonight?"

"Where are you going?"

"The general has invited me to go to the city with him. He has tickets to a show."

"Which one?" asked Taylor.

"I don't know. He wanted it to be a surprise, but he promises that I'll be pleased. Apparently, it's usually sold out." She refilled her cup with coffee. "But don't worry, girls, both Inez and Clara will be here ... in case I get home late."

DJ knew that meant that her grandmother would be quite late, and she had a feeling that Taylor suspected the same thing.

Riding to school on the Vespa actually turned out to be okay, and DJ was relieved that Taylor didn't try to knock her off going around the corners.

"Thanks for the ride," said DJ as she removed her helmet and handed it to Taylor.

Taylor set the helmets on the Vespa and then fluffed out her hair, removing her compact to check her image. She handed it to DJ. "Don't you want to make sure you don't have helmet head or bugs in your teeth?" she teased.

So, to pacify her, DJ checked. But everything seemed to be in place. She handed the compact back. "Thanks."

Taylor frowned now.

"What's wrong?" asked DJ.

She let out a sigh. "I don't know ... it just seems that no matter how hard I try to make friends, there's this barrier. Girls just don't like me. Including you, right?"

Now DJ felt guilty. Still, she didn't want to lie. "The truth is ... you can be kind of hard to like, Taylor."

"I suppose."

"And, believe it or not, I *am* trying."

Taylor blinked. "You are?"

DJ nodded.

"We better hurry or we'll be late," said Taylor. "And I've already been warned twice. I don't want to push things too far in my first week here."

So even Taylor had her limits. Still, DJ knew that Taylor's limits were primarily self-centered. As long as she came out on top, it was okay to break the rules and push the envelope. In fact, Taylor seemed to thrive on pushing everything and everyone to the max. The question was . . . why?

Still, DJ didn't have time to think about that as she hurried to English lit. Like Taylor, she didn't want to be late either. She'd had one tardy already this week and that was more than enough.

The morning seemed to flow fairly smoothly, and as DJ went to lunch—walking with Eliza and Taylor since they'd all just been in US History together—she thought that perhaps this school year was going to be a good one.

"Are those Jimmy Choos?" Taylor asked Eliza as they stood in line for lunch. As usual, they'd already staked out their table by placing DJ's bag there.

Eliza just nodded.

"Nice," said Taylor.

"Thanks," said Eliza, but the way she held her head when she said it sounded a little snotty, like she was trying to put Taylor in her place. Just then DJ noticed that Tina and Madison were looking at their saved table. And then Madison was actually picking up DJ's bag, holding it between her thumb and forefinger as if she were taking out the trash. Then she dropped it onto the floor.

"Hey, look," said DJ, nudging her friends. "They threw my bag on the floor."

"What a couple of—"

"I'm going," said DJ as she broke from the line and charged over to where Tina and Madison were now making themselves comfy at the table.

"That's *my* bag that you just threw on the floor," she told them angrily.

"That piece of crap?" said Tina. "We thought it was something the janitor forgot to take—"

"That happens to be a *Hermès* bag," said Taylor as she picked up DJ's purse and handed it to her. "Not that you small-town, fashion-challenged hick chicks would know anything about that." She looked down at Tina's blue bag. "Like what is that supposed to be? Kmart's blue light special?" Then she pointed to Madison's shiny pink bag. "And I'll bet you got a free Malibu Barbie with that little number. Is it made by Mattel?"

The girls didn't say anything.

"And you are sitting at a table that we'd saved," continued Taylor.

"It's our table now," said Madison.

"Fine," said Taylor. "Then, you'll just excuse us while we go and report what's missing from DJ's bag. We have at least three witnesses who will attest to the fact that Madison took—"

"Fine," snapped Madison, standing.

Taylor looked down on her and smiled in a very catty way. "Let me guess, Madison ... you got those pathetic jeans at Wal-Mart?"

As the two girls walked away, Taylor laughed, and DJ couldn't help but chuckle. "You are something else, Taylor."

Taylor took a twenty out of her bag and handed it to DJ. "You go and get me a salad and an iced tea, and I'll save the table."

"That's all you want?" asked DJ.

Taylor nodded. "Unlike you, I won't be sweating it out at volleyball practice after school today."

"I'm sure Coach Jones would gladly let you on the team," said DJ. "If you wanted to ..."

"Oh, yes, I'm sure she'd love me to join the team. I hear that Coach Jones likes pretty girls."

DJ rolled her eyes and headed back to join Eliza in the lunch line. Oh, well, like her grandmother had said — Rome wasn't built in a day.

"**DID Taylor make a scene?**" asked Eliza as she picked up her usual tossed green salad and lemon juice.

"Sort of . . ."

"What Taylor doesn't seem to get is that it will do her no good to make more enemies."

Suddenly, DJ remembered what she'd read about being kind to her enemies. She hadn't been very kind to Tina and Madison. Certainly, she hadn't put them down like Taylor had, but she had stood by Taylor. Wasn't that like guilt by association? Still, those girls had thrown her bag on the floor. Was she supposed to take that lying down?

"I'm putting together a plan," said Eliza quietly as they got in line to pay. "We're going to help Rhiannon get Bradford back."

"How is that even possible?" asked DJ as she balanced the tray with her food and Taylor's.

"Trust me, it's possible."

"What about how things turned out last night?" she reminded her.

"I'll admit that was sort of half-baked. But my new plan is flawless." She winked at DJ. "You in?"

DJ didn't know what to say.

"Don't tell me you're taking Taylor's side?" said Eliza. "Don't you even care about Rhiannon anymore?"

"Of course, I do. I'd do anything to help Rhiannon. What Taylor did to her was totally wrong."

Eliza smiled. "There, that's better."

"So what's your plan?"

Eliza put her forefinger over her lips. "Top secret ... for now."

"Right." DJ felt slightly compromised, but wasn't even sure why. Still, she assured herself that Eliza would never do anything mean. She just wasn't that kind of a girl. Probably she was going to give Rhiannon a pep talk and makeover and maybe work out a way to convince Bradford that he still really liked her. Something like that.

"Coming to our soccer match tomorrow?" Conner asked DJ as she was carrying her tray to the table. "It's the first home game of the year."

"What time?"

"Three."

"Hopefully, I'll be done car shopping by then."

"You're getting a car?"

"According to my grandmother, I am." She shook her head. "It's so she doesn't have to play Carter House chauffeur anymore."

"So, you'll be the chauffeur?"

"I guess."

"Still, it'll be cool having your own wheels. What're you going to get?"

"I have no idea, but Taylor offered to help me pick it out."

"You're not letting her, are you?"

"Mrs. Carter liked that idea."

"Man, I hate to think of what Taylor might pick for you. Probably a Corvette or Mustang."

"Why's that?"

"Well, my dad's always saying how those are the most dangerous cars on the road. More people get killed in them than any other car."

DJ nodded. "Okay, definitely no Corvettes or Mustangs."

"I'm pretty sure that goes for Firebirds and Camaros too."

She laughed as she set the tray on the table. "Like I'd even want any of those stupid cars. And I seriously doubt my grandmother would either. But thanks for the advice anyway."

"What kind of cars?" asked Taylor as DJ set her food and her change in front of her.

Without going into all the details, DJ explained that Conner was advising her on what kind of cars not to get.

"That's great," said Taylor, "but how about some advice on what you *should* get?"

Soon everyone at the table was giving their two cents' worth of car information to her, and by the time they exhausted the subject, she felt completely confused. "Hey, where's Rhiannon?" she asked when she noticed she was missing.

"She said she was going to spend her lunch hour finishing up an art project," said Eliza.

"Where's Bradford?" asked DJ, suddenly wishing she hadn't. What if this was part of Eliza's plan for reuniting them?

"He's with his mom," offered Taylor.

"With his mom?" said Casey.

"Yes, she's having an exhibit in her gallery tonight — he's helping her."

"That's right," said Harry. "It's First Friday."

"First Friday?" echoed Kriti. "What does that mean?"

"It means there's an art walk in town tonight," explained Taylor, like she was the expert. "All the galleries and some of the shops stay open to show the works of local artists. It happens every month on the first Friday."

"And when did you get to be so knowledgeable about local events?" teased Harry.

"I pay attention," she said. "I read the newspaper ... and ... Bradford invited me to be his guest at his mom's exhibit. That's what he's working on today. One of her regular guys was sick, and she needed to get some things up. He got excused for the afternoon."

"Lucky dude," said Harry. "Wonder if he needs any help."

Taylor shrugged. "Guess you could call and offer."

After lunch, Conner walked DJ to drama.

"We're watching the end of *South Pacific*," she told him.

"Again?"

She nodded. "Yeah, I'm sure we'll be sick of it in a few weeks."

"What part do you want?"

She laughed. "I want the part where no acting is involved—a behind-the-scenes part."

"Maybe you could do lighting."

"Or I could be the curtain puller."

They paused in front of the auditorium. "So, do you want to do the art walk with me tonight?"

"Sure."

"Maybe we could grab a bite first."

"At the Hammerhead?"

He laughed. "You poor thing. We need to make sure you get out for a high-carb, greasy, fattening meal at least two to three times a week."

She grinned at him. "You are my kind of guy, Conner."

"See ya." Then he leaned over and pecked her on the cheek.

DJ smiled to herself as she went into the auditorium. Having a boyfriend, although it took some getting used to, was kind of fun. Still, she didn't want things to get as serious as they had on that first date. She would never forget how that had really messed up their relationship.

After volleyball practice, DJ and Casey decided to walk home.

"So, you're really getting a car?" asked Casey.

"I guess so . . ."

"You don't sound too thrilled."

"Yeah, because it means I'm going to get stuck driving everyone around now."

"What about Eliza?"

"Well, she's been nice to share rides, but her grandmother isn't Mrs. Carter. And if she decides to keep her car to herself, no one can object."

"Good thing she's nice."

"Yeah."

"Unlike some people. Speaking of witches, how is it being Taylor's roommate, DJ? Were you afraid to close your eyes last night?"

"She's not that bad."

"Are you kidding?" Casey turned and stared at DJ. "She's totally evil."

"Not totally."

"Well, ninety-nine point nine percent then."

"Yeah, maybe, but I'm trying to be nice to her."

"Seriously?"

"Yeah." DJ considered telling her about the Bible verse. But how do you explain something that you don't even get yourself?

"Following Eliza's example?"

"Maybe so."

Eliza's car pulled up as they got home. She had the top down, and she and Rhiannon hopped out and waved.

"What's up?" asked DJ.

"Eliza just helped me take some of my things to the Mockingbird," said Rhiannon.

"Isn't that Bradford's mom's gallery?" asked DJ.

Rhiannon nodded and grinned.

"Gabrielle had already invited Rhiannon to display some pieces. So I helped her take them over."

"Then we stayed and helped out," said Rhiannon.

"I can't wait to email my mom that I spent the afternoon helping at Gabrielle Bruyere's gallery," said Eliza. "She'll be so impressed."

"So Bradford's mom is really a big deal?"

"Totally," said Eliza. "Plus she's really nice, and she really likes Rhiannon."

"Aha," said DJ.

Rhiannon shook her head. "No, it's not like that, DJ. I just went to help."

But Eliza winked.

"So, was Bradford around?" asked DJ innocently.

"Oh, yeah," said Eliza. "And we both just totally ignored him. We were sugar and spice to Gabrielle, but we acted like Bradford had the black plague."

"Well, I didn't ..." Rhiannon frowned.

"I did it for both of us."

Rhiannon sighed, holding out a pair of paint-stained hands. "I'm going to go get cleaned up."

Then after she went inside, Eliza continued to unveil her little plan. "Anyway, Gabrielle finally noticed that Bradford was on the outside of things, and she asked me if something was wrong."

"And?" DJ was actually getting curious now. How did girls like Eliza and Taylor know how to play these complicated games? Was there an Internet site somewhere that gave step-by-step instructions?

"And I told her about Taylor."

"What did you tell her?"

"Just the truth."

"As in?"

"I told about some of the pranks she'd played on you when she was trying to get Conner. Then I told about how she'd stabbed Rhiannon in the back to get to Bradford—those weren't my exact words, of course."

"Of course," said Casey, stifling a laugh.

"What did Gabrielle say?"

"She didn't say much, but it was clear that she didn't approve." Eliza glanced up toward the house as if she thought they were being watched and then continued in a quiet voice. "I let her know that we all think Bradford is a sweet guy, but that we're concerned that he's fallen for Taylor's tricks. I told her that I hope he doesn't get hurt. And I told her that Rhiannon has been hurt deeply, but that she's taking it like a trooper."

"Wow!" DJ just shook her head.

"You are good," said Casey with open admiration.

Eliza might be good, but DJ wasn't convinced that she was good enough to get the best of Taylor. So far DJ had witnessed no one, including herself, able to outwit Taylor Mitchell. Still, it might make for an interesting evening.

"It's the volleyball queen herself," said Taylor when DJ walked in, without knocking, of course. "Do you have a nickname on the team? Like Spike?"

"Funny," said DJ.

"Seriously, DJ." Taylor frowned at her. "How can you stand to walk home looking and smelling like that?"

DJ looked down at her gym clothes. "It beats walking home in heels. Besides I prefer the shower here to the one in the locker room."

Taylor's brows lifted. "Aha, I get it. It's Coach Jones, isn't it? Does she look at you while you're showering? I'm pretty sure she was gaping at me this afternoon, pretending to be doing office work, but I felt her looking."

"Give it a break, Taylor."

"But they say she's a dyke—"

"Puh-leeze," insisted DJ. "That's way more than enough." But even when she was in the bathroom, she could still hear Taylor making loud off-color comments, like she thought DJ was still listening and then Taylor would laugh at her own pathetic humor.

DJ drowned out Taylor as she took her time showering. Then she carefully dried her hair and put on a little makeup, finally emerging from the bathroom and hoping that Taylor might've gone outside for a cigarette or something. But there she was, sitting in the window seat and flipping through a thick issue of *Elle*. Suddenly, she held the magazine up. "Don't you think I look like this model?" asked Taylor.

"Huh?" DJ leaned over and peered at the glossy photo of a sultry-looking young woman who didn't seem to have a stitch of clothing on, although her private parts were sort of hidden within the shot. "What's she modeling anyway?" asked DJ.

"Prada perfume, but that's not the point. Don't you think I look like Kamila Klimczak's younger sister?"

"You mean that whole blue-eyed blonde thing you both got going on?"

"Not that, you moron." Taylor stood up and took the magazine over to the mirror, holding it up by her face to examine it more closely. "I mean the bone structure, stupid, the shape of the face, the slant of the eyes, the full lips—can't you see it?"

Feeling slightly bad for the blue-eyed blonde joke, DJ decided to be cooperative. She went over and stared at Taylor's face then the model's. Finally she admitted that there was a definite resemblance.

"I knew it," said Taylor, now satisfied.

"Who is she anyway?"

"Just a model from Poland." Taylor returned to the window seat and kept staring at the photo.

"Do you think you'll be a model?" asked DJ.

"Your grandmother thinks I could . . . if I wanted to . . . but I don't think I want to."

"Why not?" asked DJ. "I mean I know why I wouldn't want to, but you seem to like attention, Taylor. I'm surprised you wouldn't leap at an opportunity to model."

"It just seems pretty one-dimensional."

"Meaning it's about surface looks and not much else?"

"Pretty much."

DJ wanted to point out that Taylor was pretty one-dimensional too, but she didn't.

"Of course, the money can be good," said Taylor. "And you don't have to do it forever."

"They won't let you do it forever."

"Duh. But I suppose I could do it for a year or two—until I figured out what I really wanted to do. It might be fun."

"Not my idea of fun," said DJ as she flopped down onto her bed. "It sounds more like torture to me."

"So tell me," said Taylor. "Which of us is prettier?"

DJ sat up and frowned. "What are you talking about?"

Taylor held up the photo again. "I mean me or Kamila. Who's prettier? And be honest, I can take it."

DJ studied the photo. "Well, to be fair, I know for a fact that the photo has been airbrushed and touched up ..."

"Just pretend that I've been airbrushed too."

DJ stared at the photo then stared at Taylor. "I think it's a toss-up," she finally said. "You're both beautiful. Happy now?"

Taylor scowled.

"Well, now with that expression, I'd have to say that Kamila wins."

"What if I were a blue-eyed blonde?" asked Taylor. "Would I be prettier then?"

"Of course not." DJ firmly shook her head.

"You're just saying that."

"I'm not. I think your dark hair, dark eyes — the whole package — is really beautiful, Taylor." DJ couldn't believe she was saying this. But maybe it was because of what she'd read in the Bible today about saying good things to mean people. Whatever.

"You know that my mom is Latino," said Taylor in a slightly serious tone. "And you've probably guessed that my dad is black ..."

"Not really," admitted DJ. "I mean, yeah, I knew your mom was Latino."

"The thing is my dad doesn't look black. I mean he can pass for Latino too."

"Oh." DJ had no idea where this was going or why Taylor was even telling her. Or if it was even true. But she just nodded.

"So, when I was born, it was kind of upsetting."

"Upsetting?" DJ was just plain confused now. "Why?"

"Because I'm the darkest one in the family."

"You're not that dark," DJ pointed out. "Mostly you look like you've got a fantastic tan—one that most girls would kill for."

"Well, my dad didn't like it. Not one bit. He even accused my mom of cheating on him, you know, with someone darker."

"Seriously?"

"Uh-huh."

"Wow, that must've been hard."

Taylor shrugged. "Hard on them. I've gotten used to it."

"Do you and your dad get along?"

"You mean when he's not in rehab?"

"Yeah."

"I guess so. I mean he's gotten used to me."

Suddenly DJ realized what time it was. "Oh, I better get ready. Conner's picking me up in about half an hour."

"Going out?"

"Yeah, to eat and then that First Friday thing."

"Guess I'll see you there then."

"Guess so."

Then Taylor closed the magazine, laid it aside, and went into the bathroom. And, as DJ dressed, she tried to figure out what Taylor had just told her. Was she saying her parents didn't love her as much because her skin was darker than theirs? That just sounded crazy. Or maybe Taylor just didn't love herself. Whatever it was, it would probably take an experienced shrink a couple of years to get to the bottom of. And DJ just didn't have time.

"Thanks for dinner," DJ told Conner as they got back into his pickup.

"It's nice we have similar taste," he said.

"Well, I don't always eat cheap greasy food."

He frowned. "You mean you didn't really like it?"

"No, I totally loved it, Conner. I was kidding, okay?"

"Oh, okay."

DJ glanced at her watch. "Is it too early to go to the art walk?"

"Nah, I noticed some people were already walking around when I came by to pick you up. You know, the old-timers who can't be out too late." He drove through town and finally parked in a small lot behind The Mockingbird Gallery.

"Uh-oh," said DJ as they got inside. She pointed to the lime green Vespa parked right out the back door.

"Taylor?"

"Yep." DJ had already told Conner about Eliza's plan.

"Do you think Rhiannon is here yet?" he asked.

"I don't see Eliza's car anywhere."

"Or Harry's Jeep."

Conner pushed open the door, and the sound of jazz music floated toward them. But, other than the elderly couple admiring a bronze statue of a mother and child, the gallery looked fairly empty. Conner and DJ slowly made their way around the gallery, quietly talking about various pieces as if they were both art experts, which was so not the case. Finally the older couple left, and DJ started to giggle.

"Sorry," she said trying to control herself. "But I feel like such a phony."

"Hello and welcome to The Mockingbird," said a woman with a heavy French accent. "I am Gabrielle Bruyere."

"We're friends of Bradford, Mrs. Bruyere," said Conner, politely introducing them to her.

"But, of course." She smiled warmly. "But, please, call me Gabrielle. Or even Gabbie. And know that any friend of my son is a friend of mine."

"They're my friends too," said Taylor as she emerged with Bradford on her arm. "In fact, DJ, which is short for Desiree, is my roommate."

"Ah, Desiree, that is French," said Gabrielle.

"Yes," admitted DJ. "My mother lived in France for a while. She loved their culture and language. But I think that Desiree Jeannette is a mouthful. So I go by DJ."

"And you and Taylor are roommates? How much fun you girls must have! I can only imagine."

DJ sort of laughed. "Yes, it's pretty unbelievable."

"And you are both so beautiful. Are all the Carter House girls such rare beauties?"

Taylor chuckled. "You know what they say—beauty is in the eyes of the beholder."

"Well, I am beholding you both, and I declare you are both beautiful." Gabrielle pulled the two girls together and stared at them. "Look, boys, are they not beautiful? Such opposites . . . I would like to paint them together."

"Do you want me to put this CD in now?" asked Bradford.

"Yes, of course," said Gabrielle. She smiled at Taylor. "A signed CD from one of my favorite musicians—such a rare treat." She turned to DJ. "Your roommate has a very talented mother, no?"

"So does your son," said Taylor. "I'm still amazed at your art, Gabbie. I think I'm going to have to buy that oil of the koi pond for my mother for Christmas. It would be perfect in her bedroom."

Gabrielle clapped her hands. "A piece of my art in Eva Perez's boudoir? I could not be happier." She put her arm around Taylor and squeezed her tight. "You are so adorable!"

Just then, the sounds of Eva's deep, rich voice singing Latino jazz filled the room, and Gabrielle looked even happier. "Oh, this is going to be a wonderful evening. Desiree and Conner, you feel free to look around . . . have some wine and cheese . . . oh, wait, you cannot have any wine because you are too young." She laughed. "But we do have sparkling cider as well. Be at home, my young friends. Enjoy!"

Before long, the gallery was overflowing with visitors, and DJ started to feel claustrophobic. Eliza, Rhiannon, and Harry had arrived a few minutes ago, but DJ hadn't been able to make it over to them without risking knocking over something very valuable. Finally, she decided to resort to her cell phone. It was obvious that Eliza had spent some time dolling up Rhiannon. Her hair, clothes, and makeup had never looked better. And DJ could tell by the sparkle in Rhiannon's eyes that she had high hopes for this evening. DJ felt certain those hopes included Bradford.

"Hello?" said Eliza from across the room, although DJ could barely hear her on the phone.

"It's DJ," she said, waving past the crowd.

"Oh, there you are." Eliza waved back. "Is Bradford here?"

"Yes, but—"

"Where is he?"

"I don't know … maybe in back, but I need—"

"Do you see how great Rhiannon looks?"

"Yes, but I—"

"We'll go look for him. I think a behind-the-scenes rendez-vous is just what they—"

"Eliza," said DJ, "We need to talk."

"Of course, we do. But not like this. Gotta go, sweetie." Then she hung up.

DJ continued to wave from where she was cornered be-tween a bronze Viking statue and a barrel-chested man who smelled like tobacco. But Eliza, totally oblivious, simply waved back as she guided Rhiannon through a door that led into the back. DJ waved to Conner now. He was only about ten feet away, but there must've been three people between them. Somehow he pressed toward her.

"What's wrong?" he asked. "You look like you saw a ghost."

"Rhiannon's here. I was trying to head them off at the pass, but Eliza hung up on me."

He sighed. "Oh, DJ, there's really not much we can do. Bradford and Taylor really seem to like each other."

"But I feel so badly for Rhiannon."

"We all do, but she's going to have to get over it."

"But Eliza was so sure she could fix this."

"You girls and the games you play," he teased.

"Not me," she protested. "The only games I play usually involve balls and nets and tennis shoes."

"Wanna get outta here?"

She nodded. "Yes, please, before I pass out from lack of oxygen."

It felt wonderful to be out in the fresh air again. DJ took in a long, deep breath. "Ahh . . ."

"Want to look at any of the other galleries?"

"I don't know . . . not if they're packed like that," said DJ.

"There's one down there that probably won't be. It's not the most popular, but I like it."

"Which one?"

"The Grotto."

"The one with the fishing nets and stuff outside?"

"Yeah, it's kind of tacky, but I've always liked it. My grandpa used to bring me there when I was a kid. They only have art that's related to fishing and boats and the sea."

"Sounds good to me."

Conner was right. It wasn't crowded at all. But the owner, a tall, lanky, bald man named Jack, recognized Conner and made them both feel just as welcome as Gabrielle had done. Perhaps even more so since he actually gave them a personal tour, explaining about the various pieces and the artists who'd created them.

"And what's this you're working on?" asked Conner when they got to the back of the room where an easel was set up.

"It's called *The Burning of the Black Prince*," he said, standing back to peer at his own unfinished painting.

It was a dark painting, and although it was unfinished, DJ could see the frame of an old-fashioned ship surrounded by smoke and with orange flames shooting up and reflected on the water. "It's kind of eerie looking, isn't it?" she said and then wondered if that sounded bad. "I mean I actually get a chill down my spine when I look at it."

He grinned at her. "That's what I like to hear."

"What's it about?" asked Conner as he stared at the unsettling image.

"The Black Prince was a schooner built in the early 1800s. It was built to carry cargo, but the way it was outfitted—pierced for eighteen cannons—it was rumored the ship would make an excellent privateer."

"What does that mean?" asked DJ. "What's a privateer?"

"A ship built for battle. Back in those days it wasn't unusual for a sea town to need defense against the British. So many ports had their own privateers."

"But why was the boat burned?" asked Conner.

"I suppose it was because the English misinterpreted the purpose of the schooner. They assumed it was built for battle. Consequently, in 1814 the British raided an entire fleet in Essex, Connecticut, including the Black Prince. They destroyed twenty-eight ships, worth about a hundred million in today's dollars. Then they towed the Black Prince downriver where she got stuck in the sand. And so they burned her."

"Wow," said DJ. "That's quite a history lesson."

Jack winked at her. "Didn't know you were coming to school when you walked in here, did you?"

"Hey, I wish my US History class was half this interesting."

"You should come to class and talk sometime," suggested Conner.

Jack rubbed his chin as if considering this. Just then the bell on the door tinkled and several other art strollers walked in.

"Thanks for everything," said Conner.

"Come back and see the painting when it's finished, maybe by late next week."

"You can count on it," said DJ.

"So, what did you think?" asked Conner once they were outside.

"Cool." DJ nodded. "Very cool."

Conner took her hand and gave it a squeeze. "See, we really do like the same things."

"Hey, you two," called a guy's voice from behind. They both turned to see Harry and Eliza coming toward them. "Wanna get a cup of coffee with us?" asked Harry. "I heard there's a pretty good band playing at McHenry's."

"Sounds good to me," said Conner. "How about you, DJ?"

"Sure. I actually like McHenry's coffee better than Starbucks."

Eliza looked shocked. "Better than Starbucks?"

DJ laughed. "Yeah. But you know me, I've never been big on name brands or designers."

"My kind of girl," said Conner.

"So, what happened with Rhiannon?" asked DJ as they walked down Main Street.

"Oh, don't ask." Eliza groaned.

"What happened?" demanded DJ.

"Just tell her," urged Harry. "Get it over with so we can forget about it and have some fun, okay?"

"Fine." Eliza fell into step with DJ now. "But it wasn't pretty."

"What?" DJ was getting impatient now.

"If only I'd known what was going on ..."

"I tried to warn you," said DJ. "You hung up on me, Eliza."

"I thought it was under control. I didn't know Taylor was already there. No one saw her leave."

"Didn't you see her Vespa?"

"Where?"

"Parked in back, right by the door."

"We parked in front."

"Oh."

"Did you see how great Rhiannon looked?"

"Yes. She looked fantastic. And I could tell she felt good."

"Felt as in past tense."

"What happened?" DJ practically shouted.

"Come on," said Harry. "Just spit it out, Eliza. Or I will."

"Okay." Eliza took in a quick breath. "Rhiannon and I went into the backroom. We didn't call out or anything, but we thought we heard someone behind a closed door. We'd already seen Gabrielle out front, so we figured it was Bradford. I knocked, and then we walked in. Rhiannon first, like tah-dah, here is your dream girl. And ..." Eliza shook her head. "They were in there doing it."

"Doing *it?*" shrieked DJ in disbelief. "You mean *doing it, doing it?*"

"Yes."

"Oh no ..."

"Poor Rhiannon," said Conner.

"Where is she?" demanded DJ. "You didn't leave her there, did you?"

"No, of course, not."

"We took her home," said Harry.

"To be by herself?"

"Casey was there," said Eliza. "I called to make sure. Casey said she'd stay with her. And Kriti was supposed to be back from her little debate thing by then. Rhiannon is in good hands."

"Unlike when she was with you," said DJ bitterly.

"That seems a little uncalled for," said Eliza in a hurt tone.

"Well, you should've known better," scolded DJ.

"You should've warned me."

"I tried, remember?"

"Sooner, you should've tried sooner."

"So, it's my fault?"

"Ladies," said Harry, stepping between them like a referee. "Let's not fight about this."

"I'm sorry," DJ said to Eliza. "It's just that Rhiannon has been through so much . . . and we all know Taylor well enough to know what she's capable of. To think you could beat her at her own game, Eliza . . . well, that's just not going to happen."

"This isn't over yet," said Eliza with what sounded like steel resolve.

"It is for Rhiannon."

Eliza nodded. "Maybe, but now I'm really furious at Taylor."

"Get in line," said DJ.

"WE WEREN'T ACTUALLY DOING IT," said Taylor in an off-handed way.

DJ had waited up for her, determined to read her the riot act before she went to bed. "Yeah, right." DJ socked a throw pillow and then tossed it to her bed.

"Fine, if that's what you want to think ... sure, we were doing it, DJ. We were just going at it like a couple of sex-starved—"

"Shut up," said DJ. "If you can't be honest, just shut up."

"So, you believe me?" Taylor looked surprised. "That we weren't really doing it?"

"No, I didn't say that. I just don't want your bull."

"Believe what you want," said Taylor. "You will anyway." She pointed to DJ's Bible now. "I wonder what that book says about judging people, or misjudging them as the case happens to be here."

DJ didn't say anything. She wasn't sure what the Bible said about judging, although she'd heard Rhiannon say it was wrong. In fact, tonight when DJ and the others had sat around the living room trashing Taylor's character and plotting against her, Rhiannon had refused to participate. She'd said it was wrong, and then she'd gone to her room.

"Do you even want to know the truth, DJ? Or are you going to be one of those Christians who make it up as they go along?"

"What would you know about being a Christian anyway?" demanded DJ.

Taylor laughed. "Oh, you'd be surprised."

"I'm sure."

"Fine," said Taylor. "I'll tell you what your fat green Bible says about judging, DJ. It says 'Judge not, that you be not judged. For with what judgment you judge, you will be judged; and with the measure you use, it will be measured back to you.' Matthew seven verses one and two."

DJ blinked. "How can you possibly know that?" She grabbed up her Bible and tried to find where that section might be so that she could prove Taylor wrong, but she didn't even know where to begin.

"Here," said Taylor. "I'll show you." She took the Bible and opened it, turned several pages, and then stopped where the page was marked with the bookmark and sticky note. "Hey, it looks like you were already reading right here. Guess it didn't really sink in." She shoved the Bible back at DJ now, pointing to a section that was a little way past where DJ had just read this morning. Not that the bit about being nice to her enemies had done her much good.

DJ slowly read the sentences that Taylor had pointed out, and although the wording was slightly different, she could tell the meaning was the same. It basically said that if you judge others, you would be judged too. DJ peered at Taylor curiously. "How did you know that?"

"What difference does it make?" Taylor sat down in the window seat and picked up her magazine.

DJ closed her eyes and rubbed her temples.

"Something wrong?" Taylor asked.

"Yeah," said DJ, "you seriously make my head hurt, Taylor."

Taylor snickered. "Yeah, I get that a lot."

"Okay," said DJ, determined to try this again. "Tell me the truth, Taylor, if you and Bradford weren't *doing it*, why did Eliza and Rhiannon say that you were? Why would they lie?"

"Because they did catch us in a pretty heavy make-out session." She shrugged. "I suppose it was possible that we might've taken it further if we hadn't been interrupted . . . but I don't really think so. I actually think it would be rather tacky to have sex in the backroom of Bradford's mom's gallery, don't you think?"

"Well, of course, *I'd* think that. But I'm not you, Taylor. Sometimes you seem to have the corner on tacky."

"Thanks a lot."

"Can you deny that you've had your tacky moments?"

Taylor almost smiled. "Okay, you're right. I suppose I *have* lacked discretion from time to time."

DJ sighed loudly. "Do you have any idea of how badly you've hurt Rhiannon?"

"*Me?*" Taylor frowned. "Like I did this all on my own? What about Bradford's role? Or Eliza for that matter. I mean, what was she doing snooping around the back of the gallery like that? What was she trying to prove anyway? Rhiannon wouldn't have been hurt if Eliza hadn't been butting her nose into places it didn't belong."

"They were looking for Bradford."

"And so they found him."

"With you."

"So, that makes the whole thing my fault—and my fault alone?"

"I don't know …" DJ shook her head. "Sometimes when I talk to you, it's like I can't even think straight. You have such a gift for twisting things."

"Or maybe I just show you some different angles."

"Right." DJ pulled up her comforter now. "I'm tired. I'm going to bed."

"You're going to bed mad, aren't you?"

"Maybe. What's it to you if I'm mad? Don't I have a right to be angry?"

"I guess you don't know what the Bible says about that then do you?"

"I'm supposing you do."

"That's right. 'Do not let the sun go down on your wrath.' Ephesians four verse twenty-six."

"You are a total enigma, Taylor."

"Why, thank you, DJ. That's one of the nicest things you've said to me." Taylor removed a pair of white satin pajamas from her drawer. "But are you going to bed angry or not?"

DJ considered this. "Not."

"So, you *forgive* me?"

"Don't push it." DJ pulled the comforter over her head and groaned as if in severe pain. But she could still hear Taylor laughing after she went into the bathroom and closed the door behind her. Was it possible that DJ was rooming with the devil?

The next morning, DJ wanted to sleep in, but Inez knocked on her door at eight thirty to inform her that Mrs. Carter was waiting for her downstairs.

"Car shopping," said Taylor as she stretched sleepily. "Do I still get to come along?"

DJ frowned at her. "You really want to?"

"Sure, why not?"

DJ figured she couldn't exactly uninvite Taylor. Besides, her grandmother might expect her to come. So, without really talking, they got ready, went downstairs, had a quick breakfast, and then rode to the neighboring town of Borden. The weather was changing; clouds were rolling in off the ocean, and it felt as if rain was in the air. Hopefully, it would hold off until the guys' soccer match was over this afternoon.

"You are certainly quiet this morning, Desiree," said Mrs. Carter as she stopped at a traffic light. "Is anything wrong?"

"Just tired," said DJ from the backseat, which she had nabbed in order to avoid having to make small talk with her grandmother. Taylor had been stuck in that role, and DJ had been trying to catch a nap. "That first week of school after lazing around all summer . . . I would've liked to have slept in today."

"Well, this is something we need to take care of," said her grandmother. "I didn't want to put it off for another week."

"Where are we going anyway?" asked Taylor.

"The general recommended a car dealer to me," said Mrs. Carter as she drove through the business district. "An old friend of his. He promised to give me a good deal. The place is called Farnsworth Auto."

After a few minutes, Taylor spotted a sign, and Mrs. Carter pulled in to a good-sized car dealership. And before long they were looking at a variety of large and unimpressive cars. DJ's grandmother seemed to be under the impression that bigger was better—not surprising considering she drove a boat of a car. But every car that interested her looked like something that should belong to an old lady. And the salesman was no help since he only encouraged her.

DJ cringed as they looked at a Lincoln Town Car. "That is way too big," she told her grandmother. "And I'll bet it gets lousy gas mileage."

"I was considering it for myself," said Mrs. Carter as she ran her fingers over the shining chrome. "I would give you my older Mercedes."

DJ tossed Taylor a look that was meant to say, *help me!*

"Excuse me, Mrs. Carter," said Taylor as she stepped forward. "Do you mind if I ask why you're considering these rather large luxury cars for Desiree?"

"For safety, of course," said Mrs. Carter.

"Safety ..." Taylor nodded as if mulling this over. "But did you know that just last year, *Consumer Reports* said that Honda Civics are the safest cars for teens?"

"Really?" Mrs. Carter looked impressed. "How did you know that?"

"Because my parents were going to get me a car, and my mom did the research, and that's what she decided was safest." She smiled at the salesman now. "I'm sure you have access to *Consumer Reports* in your office, don't you? We can go online and get all this information easily."

He nodded, but his expression wasn't convincing. "You know, I do believe the young lady is right about that, Mrs. Carter. And I just happened to get in a sweet little 2006 Honda Civic as a trade-in only last week. Would you like to have a look at it?"

"And Hondas get great gas mileage," said DJ, although she wasn't positive, but it seemed a safe bet.

"That's right—up to forty miles per gallon," said Taylor.

"Really?" Mrs. Carter nodded. "Well, let's see this car."

It turned out to be a light blue, four-door sedan, complete with a sunroof. DJ actually liked it, especially after seeing the old lady cars, but she was afraid to get her hopes up. The salesman showed them all its features, focusing on the car's high safety ratings.

"This is just the kind of car that my parents would've gotten for me," said Taylor.

"It looks comfortable," said DJ, for lack of anything else to say.

"And it matches your eyes," said Taylor with a wicked grin that only DJ could see.

"Would you like to take her for a little spin?" asked the salesman.

Mrs. Carter glanced at the sign on the windshield with the price posted. "Is this the correct price?" she asked the salesman.

"Like I told you, ma'am, we post our prices at Farnsworth's, and we don't play games. What you see on the ticket is what you'll pay for the car."

"But it's so much less than the other cars we looked at."

"It's an economy car, Mrs. Carter. It's supposed to be cheaper."

Her grandmother smiled now, and DJ knew it was a sealed deal. Even so, they took it for a test drive, and both she and Taylor tried it out. They all agreed that it was a good little car. And before noon, it was purchased, and DJ and Taylor followed Mrs. Carter home in it.

"Good thing you've had your license for a year," said Taylor. "Otherwise you wouldn't be able to give anyone rides." The man who did the paperwork on the car had also given the girls the lowdown on the law regarding teen drivers, reminding them that they weren't to use cell phones while driving and telling them how many passengers they were allowed to have.

"I wonder how long Eliza has been licensed," said DJ as she turned onto the highway. "Maybe she's not supposed to have passengers—"

"I say, don't ask, don't tell."

DJ focused her attention on driving now. Not that she wasn't a good driver, but knowing this was actually her car made her want to be extra careful. "It really is a nice car," she said. "Thanks for helping to talk my grandmother into it."

"Sure."

"Was it true? What you said about safety and everything?"

"You think I'd make something like that up?"

DJ considered this. "Maybe . . ."

Taylor laughed. "You really do think I'm evil, don't you?"

DJ didn't answer that.

"For your information, it was true. My parents were going to force a Honda Civic on me, while all my other friends were driving cool cars."

"Cool cars?" DJ wondered if this meant her car was an un-cool car.

"You know, like Lexus, Audi, or even Eliza's Porsche. And I told my mom that I'd settle for an Eclipse Spyder, which is like half the price of a Porsche, but pretty cool-looking just the same. Well, she checked out the safety ratings and said, 'forget it.'"

"Oh."

"But this car is okay for you."

DJ nodded. She knew that was probably a slam. It felt like a slam. Still, she felt determined not to let Taylor spoil this. DJ had her very own car. Her first set of wheels. *Woo-hoo!*

After they got home, DJ showed her car to Casey and Rhiannon, both of whom seemed impressed. Then she offered to take them for a ride.

"No thanks," said Rhiannon.

"Come on," urged DJ. "We'll open the sunroof and—"

"I'm working on a project," said Rhiannon. "You guys go ahead and go. I'll take a ride some other time."

So DJ took Casey out and—although the clouds were still gathering—opened the sunroof, and the cool air whooshed through the car.

"Wow," said Casey, "This is so cool. We won't need to rely on your grandmother now. And no more walking home after volleyball."

"So, how's Rhiannon doing?" asked DJ as she slowed down to drive through town.

"She's pretty bummed, although she tries to act like she's not."

"I wish there was some way to cheer her up or fix this."

"After Eliza's failed attempt, I think we should all just back off."

"Yeah, I know. What a mess."

"I just wish there was a way to get back at Taylor."

DJ remembered what Taylor had said last night. "You know, it's not really fair to blame Taylor for the whole thing. I mean, Bradford is involved too. No one forced him to get involved with Taylor."

"Yeah, right. Taylor, the witch, probably put a spell on him."

"Come on," urged DJ. "Bradford is a big boy. He knew what he was doing."

"Wait a minute," said Casey suddenly. "What's up with you anyway, DJ? Have you gone over to the dark side?"

"No, of course, not. But I just think there are two sides to everything."

"How about when Taylor was going after Conner," Casey reminded her. "Did you see two sides then?"

"Maybe not . . ."

"And Rhiannon and Bradford had been together a long time."

"Well, to be fair, they'd been friends. It had only started to get serious just recently."

"Still, it was wrong. Taylor is selfish and evil and just plain mean."

"I'm not saying that Taylor was right. I'm just saying that maybe we all need to ease up ... move on, you know?"

"You *have* gone over to the dark side." Casey scowled. "Taylor's already got you in her back pocket, doesn't she?"

"No, she does not."

"Why did she go with you to get this car?"

"Because my grandmother invited her." DJ turned back toward the house now. If Casey wanted to argue, their little joy ride was about to end.

"But you could've said no. You could've refused."

"Have you met my grandmother?"

"You just wimped out."

"Fine, whatever. But for your information, Taylor was actually quite helpful with getting this car. Mrs. Carter had her eye on a Cadillac."

"Eew."

"Exactly. Taylor pointed out that a Honda Civic was a safe choice for teen drivers. She totally convinced her that it was the best car, and my grandmother believed her."

"Was it a big lie?" asked Casey as DJ pulled in front of Carter House.

"I don't think so."

"But it might've been. For all you know you're driving around in a death trap."

"I doubt that."

"But you don't know, and your problem is that you're buying into her, DJ. You are starting to trust Taylor, and that scares me!" Then Casey opened the door, hopped out, and ran into the house.

DJ leaned her head against the steering wheel and wondered how she could possibly survive the entire school year with all these girls who always seemed to be at odds with each other. Then she sat back up and smiled. Well, at least she had this little getaway car. Now, that was something!

15

stealing Bradford

THE WEEKEND PASSED QUIETLY, uneventfully even, an interesting contrast to their first week at school. DJ thought it was because, like her, they were all tired or, as in Rhiannon's case, emotionally worn out. On Saturday afternoon, DJ and Eliza had gone to the varsity soccer match, cheering Harry and Conner on even when it started to rain. They stayed until they were soaking wet and chilled to the bone, then they waved to the guys and headed home to get warm.

Taylor went out with Bradford on Saturday night. But DJ was probably the only one aware of this. That was something. At least Taylor didn't announce to everyone that they were going out. DJ also knew that Taylor was late for curfew, but apparently no one else noticed. She didn't know what time it was when Taylor finally got in, but at least she was in her bed the next morning.

On Sunday, DJ drove Rhiannon to church and sat through the service with her. But she wasn't sure what she thought of it. Some of the things the pastor said didn't quite make sense. But then there was a lot about being a Christian that didn't make sense. Like Rhiannon kept reassuring her, faith was a process. She'd have to figure it out as she went. The good thing was that DJ was still praying. And she'd been trying to read her Bible too. But it vexed her to know that Taylor knew the Bible better than she did. It made absolutely no sense. Still, DJ promised herself that the time would come when she would know it better—more than that—she would learn how to live it. She doubted that Taylor would ever figure that out.

DJ was just finishing up her assigned reading for English lit when her cell phone rang. It was Conner.

"Hey, thanks for coming to the game," he said. "Did you guys get warmed up?"

"Pretty much."

"Harry and I were totally beat afterward. We discussed asking you girls to a movie, but we were too wiped."

"Who won?"

"They did."

"Sorry."

"Yeah, it wasn't a very fun day."

"Hey, you haven't even seen my new car yet," she said suddenly.

"That's right. Why don't you come by and take me for a ride?"

"Okay." She was already standing up.

"Maybe we can get a bite somewhere," Conner suggested.

"Hammerhead's?"

"Sounds good."

So she picked him up and took him for a little spin, and he gave her two thumbs-up on her choice of vehicles.

"It's kind of weird, but Taylor actually helped to pick it out."

He suddenly grabbed the dashboard and looked around the car as if he thought it was going to fall apart. "Are you sure there's nothing wrong with it?" he teased. "No time bomb planted in the glove box?" He opened it, looked under the paperwork, and then closed it again.

"Yeah, yeah." She just shook her head. "Casey was the same way. I guess I should just keep it quiet that Taylor was involved."

"No, someone should know ... in case we need to press charges against her if you are suddenly injured in a freak car wreck."

"Whatever."

"Sorry." Conner got more serious. "It's not like you're starting to like her, are you?"

"Of course, not. I can't stand her. But I don't think everyone has to be so hard on her. She's not the only one to blame. Like she's pointed out, Bradford is a big boy. He makes his own choices. No one forced him to go with her."

"You mean it's not true?"

"What?"

"She didn't put a spell on him?"

DJ reached over and punched him in the arm. "Come on." Then she pulled up in front of the Hammerhead and turned off the car.

"Sorry. But that girl asks for it." He shook his head. "I mean, she's really a piece of work, don't you think?"

"I think she's got her issues. And I don't like a lot of things about her." DJ laughed. "Okay, I can't think of one single thing that I really do like about her."

"She is good-looking."

DJ frowned at him. "So you noticed?"

"How does a guy not notice?"

"He gouges out his eyeballs."

"Gross." He opened the door. "I'm starving."

Fortunately, they changed the subject. As they ate, they talked about the soccer match and how the refs seemed to favor the other team.

"When's your first volleyball game?" he asked as they were finishing up. Due to the weather, they were eating inside next to a window that looked out over the docks, which looked gray and gloomy today.

"Tuesday afternoon at four. Home," DJ answered.

"Cool. Count me in."

"What about soccer practice?"

"I should be able to see at least the last half."

"Since when are you so into girls' volleyball?"

"Since my favorite girl is playing."

"Well, prepare to be disappointed. We're not very good."

"You know what they say—it's not whether you win or lose, but how you play the—"

"Yeah, right. Didn't I just hear you whining about the soccer refs?"

He made a face at her as he laid enough money to cover the bill and a tip on the table. "Let's blow this joint."

The rain was starting to come down as they dashed outside and back into her car. "Where to?" asked DJ as she turned on the ignition.

"I should probably go home and attack my homework," he admitted. "I got a little behind last week, telling myself that I'd make up for it this weekend."

She nodded. "I know. I was doing some catching up myself."

So she drove him home, thanked him for dinner, and said good night. When she got to Carter House, she noticed Bradford's car parked in front. She hoped this wouldn't mean trouble. But then as she ran through the rain to the front door, she noticed he was in his car. And just as she got to the porch, Taylor emerged.

"Hey, babe," said Taylor with a grin that almost looked as if she was happy to see her. "What's up with this weather anyway?"

"You're not in Southern California anymore."

Taylor frowned now. "Does that mean that summer is over?"

"Probably not."

"You're in time for movie night."

"Again?"

"Yeah, your grandmother wants everyone to watch *Funny Face*."

"Funny Face?"

"It's an Audrey Hepburn movie about the fashion industry."

DJ rolled her eyes. "What a novel idea."

Bradford gave a little beep on his horn. "Guess I better go."

"What're you guys doing?"

"Movie."

"Have fun."

Taylor peered at DJ now. "Do you think that you and Conner will ever want to do anything with us?"

DJ shrugged, remembering how Conner had been ragging on Taylor not that long ago. "Maybe ..."

Taylor smiled. "Cool."

Then DJ went inside feeling slightly compromised. Maybe Casey was right, maybe she had gone over to the dark side. But DJ didn't think so. If anything, she was trying to do what the Bible said. She was trying to love her enemy and not judge. And it wasn't like it was easy either.

She smelled popcorn as she went inside. Following her nose, she discovered that the smell was coming from a new contraption that was set up in the living room—an old-fashioned popcorn machine that was busily popping away.

"What's this?" she asked Kriti, the only one in the room.

"Inez just set it up," said Kriti. "Mrs. Carter got it today."

"No kidding?" DJ nodded in approval.

"Of course, there will be no butter involved," pointed out Kriti. "But there's some kind of seasoning salt that's supposed to taste like butter."

DJ laughed. "That sounds about right." She looked around the deserted living room. "But where is everyone?"

Kriti shrugged. "I don't know. I just came down myself and Eliza wanted to finish up something on the computer, but I think she's coming later. The movie was supposed to start at seven."

"Maybe I'll go see if Casey and Rhiannon are coming." So DJ went upstairs, knocked on their door, and asked if they planned to join them.

"I don't think so," said Rhiannon.

"If you're worried about Taylor," said DJ. "She's not coming to the movie."

Rhiannon looked more interested now. "Well, your grandmother did say that it had to do with fashion design. I thought that sounded interesting."

"Go!" said Casey from where she was sitting on the window seat with her laptop.

"How about you?" asked DJ.

"Too much homework."

DJ tried not to look shocked. This was a new twist—Casey actually caring about homework now? Only a week ago she'd been talking about running away. "Good for you," she said.

Casey looked up from the screen with an odd expression. "Huh?"

"Good for you for staying on top of things."

"Oh, yeah. Sure." Then she went back to her screen.

Okay, DJ suspected she was just playing another one of her crazy shoot-em-up games. And maybe she was keeping the sound down so that it didn't bother Rhiannon. Whatever. "Come on," she said to Rhiannon. "There's popcorn."

"Popcorn?" said Rhiannon in an almost-happy tone.

"Yeah. But don't get too excited. No butter's involved."

"Oh."

Then DJ chuckled as they were going down the stairs. She lowered her voice. "But I could probably sneak some."

"All right! Contraband butter."

The movie was interesting in a retro kind of way. And DJ was glad to see that Rhiannon seemed to be enjoying it. Eliza came down about midway through it, but Casey remained upstairs. It was surprising how much calmer things seemed when Taylor wasn't around to stir things up. DJ suspected she wasn't the only one who'd noticed. DJ was starting to get a little bored during some long drawn-out musical scenes toward the end, and since Kriti, Rhiannon, and Eliza seemed absorbed, she decided to sneak out.

"Movie over?" asked Taylor as she came in the front door.

DJ nodded back toward the living room. "No, but it's close. It's just that I've had enough."

"Not into Fred Astaire?" she asked as they went up the stairs.

"Doesn't he seem a little old for Audrey Hepburn?"

"I know. That always bugged me too."

"You've seen it before?"

"My mom was big into old movies. I think I've seen them all."

"So how was your movie?"

"The one we thought was playing wasn't releasing until next week. So we just got coffee."

DJ was thinking it was a pretty long coffee date. And she noticed that Taylor looked a little rumpled, but she didn't mention it. They went to their room, and Taylor kicked off her shoes and flopped onto her bed. "I am so tired."

DJ took this as a hint and was actually relieved to slip into the bathroom where she got ready for bed. Maybe Taylor would be asleep by the time she went back. She didn't really want to talk to her. She didn't want to hear about the date and whether or not Taylor and Bradford really had coffee or went to some cheap hotel—not that DJ thought they had. Mostly she just didn't want to think about it or know about it. Like Taylor had said the other day, "Don't ask, don't tell." Maybe that should be their agreement as roommates.

But when DJ came out of the bathroom, Taylor, now dressed in her pajamas, looked wide awake as she sat cross-legged on her bed. "I keep smelling that popcorn," she said. "Do you think there's any left?"

DJ shrugged. "Maybe."

"I could go down and get some, but I might run into Rhiannon, and I don't think she wants to see me. I've been trying to stay out of her hair."

"So you want me to go get you some popcorn?" asked DJ.

Taylor nodded hopefully.

DJ wanted to say, *Forget it. Get your own stupid popcorn!* But at the same time, she didn't want to start a fight. Besides, what about that being nice to your enemy thing? It would be easier and quicker just to run down and get some. "Okay," she said as she went out the door. She hurried down the stairs and was surprised to see that the movie was still going. Fortunately, there was just enough popcorn remaining to fill most of a bag.

Still, she wasn't going to pilfer any butter. If Taylor wanted popcorn, she could have it dry. Besides, as Taylor was always telling her, butter was fattening.

"Thanks," said Taylor when DJ returned to their room. "That was one thing I was looking forward to tonight ... at the theater, I mean. Popcorn."

DJ sat down on her bed and picked up the book she'd been reading for English lit, pretending to be fascinated.

"Bradford is a pretty nice guy," said Taylor as she munched. "But I'm worried that he's only interested in me for one thing."

DJ just nodded, wishing that Taylor would shut up.

"I'm sure some people wouldn't believe me, but I don't want a guy who's only into having sex. I want a guy who appreciates me for my mind as well."

DJ controlled herself from laughing.

"I know that you're sitting there thinking I'm full of it," said Taylor. "Aren't you?"

DJ looked up from her book. "Yeah, sort of."

"And why is that?" Taylor narrowed her eyes at DJ.

"Maybe you should have someone sneak around and film you, Taylor, so you could see how you come across sometimes."

"Meaning?"

"Meaning, you come across as ... as a *man-eater!*"

"A man-eater?" Taylor laughed. "What is that supposed to mean?"

"That's what Conner called you."

She frowned. "When?"

"I don't know ... a while back. But he thinks you're trouble. As a guy, his perception of you is a girl who wants to trap a guy, chew him up, and spit him out. I'm pretty sure he said something like that."

She made a face. "He's probably just jealous."

"Jealous?" DJ laughed. "He had his chance with you, Taylor. Remember? He was *not* interested."

"Or maybe he was just afraid."

"Afraid of what?" asked DJ.

She shrugged. *"A man-eater."*

"Yeah, whatever."

"Sometimes I wish I could be like you." Taylor went on.

DJ looked up again. "What does that mean?"

"You know, just ordinary."

DJ rolled her eyes.

"I don't mean ordinary in a bad way. I mean just a normal girl . . . doing normal stuff—none of this baggage."

"Did you ever stop to think that you create your own baggage, Taylor?"

"Maybe . . . sometimes . . . but you don't know everything about me."

"And you don't know everything about me either. Yet you think I'm so ordinary—so normal. You don't know what I've been through."

"I know your mom died." She sighed. "Sorry."

DJ just nodded and, surprisingly, felt a lump in her throat.

"I don't know what I'd do if my mom died. I mean, I act like I hate her sometimes, but I don't. I just hate some of the things she does."

"Like what?" DJ was actually curious now. This was the most personal thing Taylor had ever revealed about herself and her family.

"I hate that she puts up with my dad."

"Puts up with him? How?"

"All kinds of ways. His drinking for one thing. His abuse."

"He's abusive?"

"When he's drunk."

"To your mom?"

Taylor shook her head and looked down at her lap. "No. He's good to my mom."

"Who's he abusive …" But even as DJ said it, she knew.

Taylor shook the last kernels of popcorn into her hand and just stared at them.

"Your dad's been abusive to you?"

She just shrugged.

"Does your mom know?"

"Oh, yeah … she knows."

DJ felt like she was in way over her head now. It wasn't as if she was a counselor or a shrink or anything. On the other hand, Taylor was opening up to her. Unless this was a trick. Was Taylor making this up just to win DJ's sympathy? "So, if your mom knows, why does she put up with it?"

"She loves him." Taylor looked up with an impossible-to-read expression. "Obviously more than she loves me."

"Oh."

"That's why I'm here."

DJ nodded.

"I probably shouldn't have told you all that." Taylor looked worried now. "But for some crazy reason, I trust you."

"It's okay," said DJ. "I won't tell anyone."

Then without saying anything more, they both finished getting ready for bed and turned out the lights. And once she was under her comforter, DJ prayed for Taylor. For real this time.

STEALING BRADFORD

TWO CARS LEFT THE CARTER HOUSE for school on Monday morning. Four girls rode with Eliza. But Taylor was DJ's only passenger. And she had a strong feeling that wasn't a coincidence. It seemed like everyone was punishing Taylor now. Well, except for DJ. Not that she wasn't still aggravated at Táylor, especially for Rhiannon's sake, but that earlier sense of outrage had pretty much evaporated.

"They're freezing me out," said Taylor as DJ drove them to school.

"I don't know."

"You do too know." Taylor reached for her bag, taking out her cigarettes.

"Not in my car," warned DJ.

"I'll open the window."

"No." DJ turned and gave her a look to show she meant it.

"Fine. Whatever." Taylor scowled darkly now.

"Why do you smoke anyway?" asked DJ.

"Why not?"

"Don't you care about your lungs?"

"My lungs are fine."

175

"Right, now ... maybe ... but what about later? What if you were going to have a singing career like your mom, but you couldn't because of smoking?"

"My mom used to smoke."

DJ considered this. "Used to ... so she had the sense to quit, right?"

"Yeah."

"My point."

"Look, DJ. I'm sure you mean well, but you are getting on my nerves, and that just makes me want to smoke."

So DJ attempted to change the subject, asking about whether Taylor had a specific role she wanted to try out for in drama.

"Probably."

"Which one?"

"I'd say Nellie, but I have a feeling Eliza will bag that one."

"Eliza does seem like a Nellie," agreed DJ.

"You mean all that perky, blue-eyed blonde stuff? Well, don't kid yourself, I could wear a wig and makeup."

"You really think you can pull off cheerful and happy?"

"It's called *acting*."

"So, you're trying out for Nellie then?"

"No. I'm not stupid."

"What?"

"Probably Liat. That seems the obvious choice."

DJ nodded. "Well, you'd be a good Liat. You could even pass for Polynesian. And you wouldn't need a wig or anything."

"And she's got some good songs."

"And you've got a nice voice."

"How do you know?" Taylor asked.

"I heard you in the shower the other day. You were good."

"Thanks."

DJ barely had the car in park before Taylor jumped out and lit a cigarette. So much for DJ's distraction tactics.

"I'm going to class," DJ said.. "Enjoy the fresh air."

"Thanks." Taylor rolled her eyes as she blew out a long puff of smoke.

DJ looked for Eliza and the other girls, spotting them just as she reached the entrance. "Hey, wait," she called, hurrying to join them.

"Sorry you got stuck with her," said Eliza as they gathered at the top of the steps.

"That's okay."

"She's such a witch," said Casey. "I don't know how you can stand her, DJ. I mean you not only room with her, you get stuck driving her too. Why didn't you make her walk or take her Vespa?"

DJ just shrugged.

"I'm glad you're being nice to her," said Rhiannon.

"Really?" DJ felt relieved.

"Of course. That's the right thing to do."

"That's nuts," said Casey.

"Hey, I really appreciate that you guys care about me," said Rhiannon. "But I'm ready to move on, okay?"

"That seems wise," said Kriti. She smiled at Rhiannon. "What's that saying? There are a lot of fish in the ocean?"

Rhiannon nodded. "Definitely."

"So that's it?" said Casey. She looked disappointed. "Taylor wins?"

"She's not winning," said Rhiannon.

"Yes, she is," said Casey. "You act like her doormat, and she gets away with being a selfish witch and then ends up with Bradford too?"

"That's not winning," said Rhiannon.

"I don't get that," said Casey.

"I think Rhiannon is saying that it's not over until it's over," said Eliza.

"Here she comes now," warned Kriti.

Suddenly, they were all scattering and only DJ remained.

"They are so immature," said Taylor. "Can't they just get over it?"

"I'm sure they will," said DJ as they went into the building. "In time."

"Hey, Taylor," called Bradford, waving as he approached them.

"Hey," said Taylor. Her previous scowl amazingly turned into a brilliant smile as he slipped an arm around her waist.

"What's up, Babe?" He looked at her like she was a goddess, and she literally beamed. DJ wanted to hurl.

"See you guys," DJ said, eager to escape this embarrassing display of stupidity. She wasn't totally opposed to expressing affection in public, but she was one of those girls who thought less was more. Fortunately, Conner seemed to be of a similar mind. But maybe they should discuss this before long, just in case it ever became an issue.

As usual, Monday morning dragged. And as DJ was heading for fourth period, all she could think about was lunch.

"Hey, DJ," called Conner as he jogged to catch up with her. He had a hard-to-read expression on his face—something like concern mixed with amusement. "Have you seen it yet?"

"Seen what?" she asked.

"The photos on *MySpace dot com*."

"Huh?"

"Taylor."

"What are you talking about?"

"I can't go into the details now, but get ahold of a laptop and check this out." He handed her a slip of paper with a website address. "I gotta run. I'm late already."

DJ shoved the paper into her pocket and headed for US History. Eliza was just sitting down, and DJ took the seat beside her.

"What's up?" asked Eliza.

DJ shrugged. "Not much, although Conner just told me I need to check out some website." She stood up and dug in her pocket to remove the slip of paper. "Something about Taylor."

Eliza leaned over to look at the paper. "Oh, that's just her MySpace site. What's the big deal? I mean, besides being tacky."

Taylor walked into class just then, frowned at Eliza and DJ, and sat down, carefully crossing one long leg over the other as if to remind them that even if everyone hated her, she was still gorgeous. Not that DJ hated her; she didn't. But being with Eliza probably sent the message that she did.

Mr. Myers handed out a printout and briefly explained that they would be doing research projects this week. They were to choose a partner and pick a subject from the printout. The first three days of the week would be used for research time, and the paper would be due on Friday.

"Be my partner," said Eliza with a big smile.

"Sure," said DJ, relieved that she wouldn't be stuck with Taylor, but then guilty for being relieved.

"Let's go to the computer lab," said Eliza. Mr. Myers signed a pass and they left.

Once they were settled at a computer, Eliza immediately punched in the MySpace address, and a rather provocative and somewhat skanky-looking photo of Taylor popped up.

"Well now," said Eliza. "What exactly is Taylor up to? Training to become a porn queen?"

DJ quickly read the text, which was supposedly written by Taylor, but somehow didn't ring quite true to DJ's ears. For one thing, there were dumb typos and bad grammar mistakes, and it just sounded plain stupid, which everyone knew Taylor was not.

Eliza clicked on the spot that said "see more," and suddenly there was a photo of Taylor and a girl with short blonde hair in a tight embrace and kissing each other on the lips.

"Eew," said Eliza. "That is seriously twisted!" She turned and stared at DJ now. "Is Taylor gay?"

"Of course not." But even as DJ said this, she had no idea.

"Okay, bisexual. Is she bi?"

"I don't know."

Then Eliza clicked onto more photos, which were even more explicit and nauseating. All featured Taylor as the star—and all with other girls.

"This is so sick," said DJ.

"Totally messed up," said Eliza as she clicked onto another.

"Turn it off," said DJ as she stared with a mixture of shocked fascination, horror, and disgust.

"I can't believe you're sharing a room with that pervert."

"What is that?" demanded Taylor from behind them.

DJ tried to cover up the screen with her hands, but Taylor leaned over and pushed her aside.

"I'm sure you've seen it before," said Eliza. "We should be asking you what it is."

Taylor's dark eyes got huge as she stared at the horrid photos. And, as if wanting to give her the whole virtual tour, Eliza clicked onto each of them again, including the kissing scene. By now there was a small crowd watching over their shoulders, and some of the guys began hooting and whistling and making crude remarks.

"That's enough," said DJ, reaching over and turning the screen off. The boys made disappointed moans.

"I've got the website address," said one, as he headed over to another computer, trailed by a group.

DJ turned and looked at Taylor now, curious as to how she would explain this. But she couldn't have been more surprised when she saw tears streaming down Taylor's cheeks. DJ had never seen her cry.

"Those are *not* of me," said Taylor.

"They sure looked like you," said Eliza in a skeptical tone. "And your name is all over the site."

"That's not me!" She wiped the tears off of her cheeks. "Someone went to a lot of trouble to set this up." She stared at Eliza and DJ now, looking from one to the other. "Did you guys do this?"

"No way," said DJ. "This is disgusting."

"Eliza?" demanded Taylor. "I know you hate me. Is this how you take your revenge?"

"You've got to be kidding." Eliza looked offended. "This is totally slimy. I would never be caught dead doing—"

"But you could've hired someone to do it for you," said Taylor quickly. "We all know you could afford it and you—"

"I had absolutely nothing to do with this," said Eliza. She stood now and looked Taylor right in the eyes. "I swear I didn't. This is really low-down and skanky, and I would never—"

"Fine," snapped Taylor. "I actually believe you. And I'm pretty sure DJ didn't do it either."

Laughter came from where the boys were now ogling the computer screen on the other side of the room, followed by more hoots and lewd remarks.

"What am I going to do?" whispered Taylor. This was the first time DJ had seen Taylor on the defense and actually looking scared.

"Get it taken down," said DJ.

"Sue someone," added Eliza. Then she shook her head. "Although it's your own stupid fault, Taylor. You never should've allowed those photos to be taken."

"I said they're not of me!" yelled Taylor.

"Yeah, right," called a guy from the other computer. "But, hey, we think you're hot."

"Totally hot," said another guy.

Taylor's eyes filled with tears again and then without saying another word, she turned and ran from the room. DJ considered going after her, but wasn't sure what she could say or do to make this any less painful.

"So Taylor gets to find out how it feels to be hurt for a change," said Eliza smugly.

"Did you have this done?" demanded DJ, suddenly suspicious.

"No." Eliza sighed. "Like I already said, this is way below me. I would never stoop to something as nasty and creepy as this."

"Well, I honestly don't believe that's Taylor's site."

"No, of course not."

"Who did it then?"

"Rhiannon would be suspect," said Eliza. "Except that I'm pretty sure she's next in line for sainthood."

"Rhiannon would never do something like that."

"Unless she has another side." Eliza smiled. "Some religious people are like that. They act all holy and good, and then when no one is looking they —"

"Shut up," said DJ.

"Well." Eliza looked truly offended now.

"Sorry," said DJ. "But Rhiannon is not like that."

Eliza shrugged. "People are full of surprises, DJ. The sooner you figure that out, the smarter you'll be."

"Whatever." DJ pulled out their assignment sheet and tried to act like she was researching—anything to keep her mind off the nasty business with Taylor. Who had done it? An enemy from California? And how did Conner find out about it? Furthermore, and perhaps more worrisome, did he look at those photos too? *What was wrong with people?* DJ wondered as she scanned the image of an old newspaper. Why would someone go to such lengths to hurt someone else?

TAYLOR WASN'T ANYWHERE TO be seen at lunchtime. Not that DJ blamed her. She couldn't even imagine how she would react if something like this had happened to her. Naturally, it was the hot topic at their table.

"Were those photos really of her?" asked Bradford with a seriously freaked expression.

"We wanted to ask you the same thing," teased Harry. "You've probably seen more of Taylor than anyone here."

"Shut up," said Bradford.

"Where's Rhiannon anyway?" asked Kriti. "I haven't seen her since this morning."

"Do you think Rhiannon could have done this?" asked Harry.

"No way," said DJ.

"Absolutely not," added Bradford. "Rhiannon is not that kind of a girl."

"I'd have to agree," said Conner. "That is totally out of character for her."

"Who then?" asked Bradford, glancing around the table with suspicion.

DJ noticed that Casey was being unusually quiet during lunch. And she couldn't help but remember how Casey had been extra protective of Rhiannon lately, almost acting as if Taylor had offended her as much as she had hurt Rhiannon.

"How did everyone find out about the website?" asked DJ.

"Good question," said Eliza. "I found out from you, DJ."

"And I got the address from Conner."

"Harry showed me the site in chem class," said Conner.

"I saw it there too," admitted Kriti with a severe frown. "Not that I wanted to see it. But the whole class was looking while Mr. Skinner was out."

"How did you find out about it, Harry?" demanded Eliza.

"The same way most of the guys in school found it," he said. "In the restroom. Someone taped a poster on the wall."

"A poster?" DJ tried to imagine this.

"Not a poster-poster. It was just a piece of white paper with a photo of Taylor, obviously taken from the website. Then at the bottom were these tear-off pieces for the address so that it would be easy to find online. It reminded me of those posters you see on bulletin boards, like someone selling a car or looking for a roommate."

"This person is slick," said Eliza.

"You mean sick," said DJ.

They continued to kick it around and speculate, but no conclusions were made. And no accusations either, although DJ was getting more and more suspicious of Casey.

"How do we get it shut down?" asked DJ as they started to leave.

"Why bother?" asked Harry. "I'm sure the whole school has seen it by now anyway."

"Because it's wrong," said DJ.

"It is wrong," added Kriti. "Not to mention cruel."

"That's right."

"But it's not really your problem," said Casey, probably the first thing she'd said during the lunch hour.

"Not my problem?" demanded DJ. "Taylor happens to be my roommate. I'd say that it's a little bit my problem."

"Has she been coming onto you?" teased Harry.

"No," said DJ, now flustered. "But she's hurting."

"Yeah, right," said Casey. "That girl has a heart of stone."

"She was crying today," said DJ, "when she saw the photos."

"Really?" Kriti actually sounded concerned now.

"She was," admitted Eliza. "It surprised me too."

"Well, maybe it's about time she got some of her own medicine," said Casey.

"I can't believe you, Casey," said DJ. "I'd think you'd know how it feels to be hurt like that. I'd think you'd have a little more empathy."

Casey shrugged. "You know what Eliza said—what goes around comes around."

DJ just shook her head as she stared at her old friend. Then she turned away from the group and headed straight toward the office. Taylor might be mean and selfish, but she didn't deserve this. No one did.

"I'd like to see Mrs. Seibert," she told the receptionist.

"Do you have an appointment?"

"No, but this is an emergency."

"Let me see if she's back from lunch."

DJ had to wait about five minutes, but she was eventually allowed in the counselor's office. She quickly explained her dilemma, and Mrs. Seibert took careful notes and finally, using her own computer, checked out the website.

"Oh my!"

"Yeah, pretty disgusting, isn't it?"

"Let me make some calls," she said quickly. "We'll see what it takes to shut that thing down, and then I'll get some legal advice." She picked up the phone and then turned to DJ. "Do you know who might've done this?"

DJ considered the question and then just shook her head. She knew she couldn't accuse Casey. She honestly didn't have a shred of evidence; it was only a hunch. Hopefully, she was wrong. But even if she discovered that Casey was the creator of this mean hoax, DJ didn't know if she could turn her in.

"Thank you for coming forward with this information," said Mrs. Seibert as DJ stood. "I've heard of incidents like this before, but never in our school. I guess it's about time we created a harassment policy that covers the Internet."

DJ nodded. "Yeah, that's probably a good idea."

"Pick up a note from the receptionist to excuse you for being late to class."

"Thanks."

By the time DJ got to drama class they were in the midst of auditions. Eliza was onstage and doing a pretty good job of singing "I'm Gonna Wash that Man Right Out of My Hair." Not surprisingly, Taylor was nowhere to be seen. DJ had already tried Taylor's cell phone, which went straight to messaging. DJ took a seat in the back of the auditorium, wondering if there was something more she should do. Was there someone else she should contact? Her grandmother perhaps? But what good would that do? Maybe it was best to simply wait for this whole thing to blow over.

"How are you doing?" whispered Rhiannon as she slipped into the seat next to DJ.

DJ shrugged. "Frustrated."

"You mean because of the thing about Taylor and the photos?"

"Have you seen it?"

"Barely. I could hardly stand to look."

"I just got through telling the counselor. They're going to try to get it shut down."

"Taylor didn't really post those herself, did she?" asked Rhiannon.

"No, of course not. She might be selfish and thoughtless, but she's not an idiot."

"I actually feel sorry for her."

"Me too."

"Do you think she's coming for auditions?"

"I think she's got other things on her mind."

"Mr. Harper suggested I try out for the role of Liat, but I think it's only because I'm short."

"Do you want to?"

"Maybe ... but I don't know if I can pull it off."

DJ flipped one of Rhiannon's red curls. "Maybe with a wig."

"And makeup."

DJ considered mentioning that Taylor had planned to audition for Liat, but then she wondered why bother bringing it up? For all DJ knew, Taylor might not want to live here now. With almost everyone turned against her and people making fun of her, she might be on her way back to California right now.

The afternoon seemed to go more slowly than usual, and in seventh period Taylor wasn't in PE. Not that this surprised DJ. But it did concern her. Everyone was still talking about the photos and making tacky jokes at Taylor's expense. Even during volleyball practice, some of the girls, including Casey, took their potshots at her. Then, as DJ drove them home after practice, she actually quizzed Casey to see if she might've been involved.

"Come on," she urged Casey. "Just come clean if you did it."

"I don't see why you even care who did it," Casey told her. "Taylor deserved it, didn't she?"

"That's not the point. Were you involved?"

"What difference does it make who was involved?"

"I just want to know."

"What's going on here, DJ?" demanded Casey. "Are you feeling sorry for Taylor now?"

"I just think that it was wrong to do that—I mean, to use MySpace to hurt someone like that."

"How about how Taylor hurt Rhiannon? Was that right?"

"No, but—"

"I don't get you, DJ. You act like you care about Rhiannon, and then it's like you're obsessed with helping Taylor."

"I just wanted to know if you were involved."

"It feels like you're turning against me." Casey let out an exasperated sigh.

Of course, Casey's defensiveness only increased DJ's suspicions. Not that she'd know what to do if she discovered that Casey was the culprit. Still, she felt badly for Taylor. And when she got home, she felt somewhat reassured to know that the other girls at Carter House were starting to feel a little uneasy about Taylor too.

"So you guys didn't see her at all this afternoon?" Eliza asked DJ and Casey.

"Not since US History," said DJ. "Same as you."

"Maybe you should check in your room," suggested Kriti. "See if it looks like she's packed up or taken anything."

"Good idea," said DJ. "It had occurred to me that Taylor might've called her mom and gotten on the next flight to LA. By the way, has anyone mentioned this to Mrs. Carter yet?"

They all said no.

"We thought we'd leave that to you," said Eliza.

"Thanks a lot," said DJ. Then she went to check in their room. But everything looked pretty normal—no signs that Taylor had taken anything. All her things seemed to be in place.

"How about her Vespa?" asked DJ when she came out of her room. "Did you check to see if it's still here?"

"Good idea," said Rhiannon.

So they all hurried downstairs and went outside to look, but the Vespa was gone.

"It's not very nice motor-scooter weather," pointed out Kriti. The sky was dark with clouds now, and a few raindrops were just beginning to fall.

"I'm going out to look for her," announced DJ. "If I'm not back in time for dinner, make an excuse to Mrs. Carter for me." As she went upstairs to get her bag and her keys, she hoped that someone might offer to join her in the search. But no one did. Although they did seem somewhat curious as to Taylor's whereabouts, DJ didn't get the sense that they were overly concerned with her welfare. And perhaps she shouldn't be either. If anyone could take care of herself, it was Taylor. But then DJ remembered that sad, lost look on Taylor's face today. And she remembered what Taylor had confided to her last night. And, despite not wanting to care, she was worried.

"I'll be praying for you," said Rhiannon as DJ came down the stairs. "I'd come with you, but if you found Taylor, she might prefer that I wasn't around, you know?"

DJ nodded. "You're probably right." So she got in her car and drove around town, checking at the coffee shops and even the nearby mall, and finally along the docks and down by the beach, but she didn't spot the lime green Vespa anywhere.

She tried Taylor's phone again and, as before, it went straight through to voicemail. Either Taylor's battery was dead or her phone was turned off. By the time DJ got home, it was raining hard.

"Don't worry, DJ, she's probably perfectly fine," said Eliza as she and the other girls met DJ in the foyer to find out whether or not she'd had success.

"Probably holed up in some cozy spot just wanting to get everyone all worked up and freaked out," added Casey.

"Or maybe she did fly home," said Rhiannon hopefully. "Maybe she'll send for her things later."

DJ hoped they were right. The image of Taylor riding around in the rain on her Vespa seemed pretty dismal, not to mention dangerous.

"Where is Taylor?" asked Mrs. Carter when everyone was seated at dinner.

All the girls admitted that they didn't know, and then Mrs. Carter simply shrugged. "I do not mind if you girls miss dinner. I only ask that you exercise good etiquette and let us know accordingly."

Dinner was unusually quiet, and DJ wondered if they were all waiting for her to tell Mrs. Carter the news. But DJ had already decided that it would be best to wait until after dinner. Plus, that would give Taylor more time to get back, that is if she planned to return.

"May I speak with you privately?" DJ asked her grandmother as the table was finally beginning to clear.

Mrs. Carter looked surprised and then nodded yes.

When they were both seated in her office, DJ told her grandmother the whole story, starting with the boyfriend-stealing incident, the website smut, and eventually, the fact that Taylor and her Vespa both seemed to be missing.

"No one has seen her since noon," DJ finally admitted.

"Oh my." Mrs. Carter looked seriously worried now. "Do you think she's all right, Desiree?"

DJ considered this. "Probably, but I don't know for sure. She did seem upset."

"Where could she possibly be?"

"I drove all over town looking for her, and I've tried her cell phone several times, but she's not answering."

"Do you think I should call the police?"

DJ wasn't sure what to say. "How about calling her mother first?"

Mrs. Carter sighed deeply. "I don't know . . . I hate to alarm her if it's nothing."

"I actually wondered if Taylor might've called her mom already," said DJ. "Maybe she's on a flight home right this minute."

"Goodness, I hope not. But surely her mother would've informed me if that were the case."

"You'd think so."

"I don't believe one can file a missing person report unless the person has been gone for twenty-four hours."

DJ felt shocked. "Are you really going to call the police?"

"Not tonight."

"But what about her mother? She has a right to know." DJ felt extremely frustrated now. Why didn't her grandmother know this? And why was DJ feeling so responsible now? This wasn't really her problem. It was her grandmother who was responsible for the welfare of the girls who were under her care. Didn't she get it?

"I suppose . . ." Still Mrs. Carter didn't seem convinced.

"Look," said DJ with all the authority she could muster. "If something is wrong, like if Taylor's been in an accident or something, and you don't call her mother, don't you think she'll be angry?"

"Yes, I suppose so."

"Or, if Taylor is on her way home, wouldn't you like to know before you embarrass everyone by calling the police?"

"Yes, Desiree, you are probably right. I will call her mother immediately. Thank you."

DJ took this as her cue to leave, but because she felt invested in this dilemma, she decided to stay. "Go ahead and call her," she said. "I don't mind waiting." And she waited as her grandmother looked up the number and finally called. She could tell she was uncomfortable dispensing such unfortunate information, but, as always, she handled it gracefully and carefully, and DJ could tell by her responses that Taylor's mother had no idea what was going on or where Taylor might be.

"Of course, Eva. And I'll let you know as soon as she comes in. Yes, you are probably right. I'm sure she's simply taking some time to cool off." She paused to listen. "Yes, I understand how teen girls can be. It's a difficult time." Then she thanked her and hung up.

"So, she's not on her way home?"

"Apparently not."

"But her mom's not too concerned?"

"She said that Taylor's been known to take off like that before when something upsets her. But she always comes back."

"Oh."

"Don't worry, Desiree." Mrs. Carter stood now. "I'm sure she's perfectly fine. Probably at a friend's house."

"A friend?" DJ tried to imagine who could be Taylor's friend. Then she thought of Bradford and his mother. Maybe Taylor was with them. Back in her room, DJ tried his number, and he admitted that he hadn't seen her since morning.

"And you haven't talked to her on the phone?"

"I left a message."

"Oh."

"I told her that I thought it was best if we broke up. I don't think it was really working anyway."

"Really?" Now, despite everything, this made DJ really angry. Talk about flaky!

"I know what you're thinking, DJ. But the truth is Taylor was probably too much for me. I mean she's fun and smart and everything, but she sort of makes my head spin, you know? I've actually already talked to Rhiannon about this. She seems to understand."

"Meaning?"

"Meaning Rhiannon and I are getting back together."

DJ couldn't help but let out an exasperated sigh.

"You're not on Taylor's side now, are you?" asked Bradford.

"It's not about sides," she said in a tired tone. "This isn't a war."

"No, I didn't mean that."

"Well, if by any chance you hear from Taylor, will you let me know?"

"Sure. But I doubt that she'll be calling me."

"Right." Then she told him good-bye and hung up.

DJ STAYED UP PRETTY LATE, praying for Taylor and asking that God would bring her safely back to Carter House, but she eventually fell asleep. When she woke up, it was morning and Taylor was still not home. It was pretty early, but DJ knew she wasn't going back to sleep anyway. So she got up, showered and dressed, and then went to speak to her grandmother in her bedroom. DJ could tell she'd awakened her, but she didn't care. Something needed to be done now.

"Taylor didn't come home last night?" said Mrs. Carter as she tied the belt of her satin robe.

"No. And I think you should call the police immediately," said DJ in a firm voice. "For all we know, Taylor could've gotten into a wreck on her Vespa. Maybe she's lying in a ditch right now with a broken leg and hypothermia."

"Yes, yes . . . you may be right."

DJ folded her arms as she waited for her grandmother to look up the number and phone the police. She explained the situation and then answered their questions. With the help of DJ, she gave them the information. Still, it wasn't easy to hear Taylor described like that, as if her grandmother were giving details that might later be used to identify the victim of a crime scene. DJ shuddered as her grandmother hung up.

"Now I suppose I should call her mother."

"Definitely," said DJ.

"Oh dear." Mrs. Carter shook her head. "Perhaps boarding teenaged girls is not such a good idea after all."

DJ wanted to shout, *Duh!* but controlled herself. Instead she just shook her head and left the room.

The talk at school quickly shifted from the nasty photos on the website to the missing girl. Everyone began to speculate as to Taylor's whereabouts, and the stories grew grimmer and more depressing as the day went by.

"Maybe she drove her Vespa off the end of the dock," said Conner.

"Maybe she was kidnapped by some perv who saw her photos and wanted to sell her as a sex slave," suggested Harry dramatically. Eliza gave him a sharp elbow and a warning glance.

"Maybe we should all just quit talking about it," said DJ with irritation. "In fact, if you want to do something really helpful, maybe we should all be praying for her."

"That's right," said Rhiannon.

Well, that shut everyone up, and DJ didn't care if she'd offended anyone. She stood up and walked away from the table. If they wanted to keep manufacturing these pathetic stories, that was their problem, but she did not have to stick around and listen. For the umpteenth time, she tried Taylor's cell phone again.

"I know you're probably not even checking your messages," she said hopelessly. "But I just wanted you to know that I'm thinking of you, and I'm praying for you. I really do care about you, Taylor, and I hope you're okay. And, you probably won't believe this, but I actually miss you and was starting to look forward to being your roommate. Please call." Then she hung up.

"You've really changed," said Rhiannon as they walked to drama together.

"How?" asked DJ dejectedly.

"You care about people."

DJ turned and looked at Rhiannon with surprise. "Meaning?"

"Meaning, I can see God at work in you. I can see him changing you."

"Really?" suddenly DJ felt a spark of hope. "You can actually see that?"

"Oh yeah. And not just me. A couple of the kids at lunch mentioned it too, after you left."

"In a good way?" asked DJ. "Or were they making fun of me?"

Rhiannon laughed. "Well, both, to be honest."

"It figures."

"But some of them came to your defense."

"Who?"

"Conner, of course."

DJ smiled.

"And Kriti and Eliza too."

"That's nice, not that I care what they think. I mean I sort of care. But mostly I'm worried about Taylor right now. I hope she's okay."

"Me too."

"I just tried her phone again."

"Nothing?"

DJ nodded sadly.

"She's probably okay," said Rhiannon as they went into the auditorium. "You can't really blame her for wanting to lay low after those photos."

"I hope that's all it is."

"I bet she'll be at Carter House by the time we get home."

"Yeah, you're probably right."

But Rhiannon was wrong. By the time DJ and Casey got home, not only was Taylor still not there, but the police were now waiting to speak to them.

"We've questioned everyone else," said Detective Howard as he led them into Mrs. Carter's office. "Now, we'd like to speak to you two, if you don't mind."

"That's fine," said DJ. For no explainable reason she felt a little nervous. But as she sat down, she noticed that Casey looked more than a little nervous. In fact, she looked down-right frightened.

"Mrs. Carter already gave us permission to search your room," he said to DJ. "I hope you don't mind."

"Not at all."

"So when was the last time you saw Miss Mitchell?" he asked them, and they both said it had been the previous morning at school. Then he went through some more fairly ordinary-sounding questions about friends and boyfriends and Taylor's emotional state and whether or not she had said anything that suggested she planned to take off. After about twenty minutes he was done.

"I appreciate your help with this," he told them politely. "I know it's hard on all you girls. It's always frightening to have a friend go missing. But in most of these cases, it turns out to be a runaway situation. And, after what I heard from the school about the Internet prank, it's understandable. I'm sure Miss Mitchell will be back soon." Then he closed his book.

"And as far as the Internet prank?" said DJ. "Is that under investigation too?" She restrained herself from looking at Casey now.

"We're considering it as possibly being related to this, although it's not easy to track these things on the Internet — and the website was already down by the time we learned of Miss Mitchell's disappearance. However, we will put a computer expert on it."

"Good," said DJ. "Whoever did it should bear some responsibility in this."

He nodded. "I have to agree with you on that." Then he thanked them for their time and left. But DJ remained in her grandmother's office. As did Casey.

"I know what you did," said DJ in a solemn tone.

Casey just nodded.

"But I don't know what to do about it."

Two streams of tears slid down Casey's cheeks. "I'm ... I'm sorry," she said quietly.

"Why?" demanded DJ. "Why on earth would you do something like that? Something so totally stupid and mean and creepy?"

"I don't know."

"Of course, you know, Casey. *Tell me why.*"

"Because I hated her!" Casey looked up at DJ with watery eyes. "I hated her, and I wanted to punish her for what she did to Rhiannon."

"What would Rhiannon think if she knew what you did to Taylor?"

Casey looked down. "I don't know."

"Yes, you do, Casey. Don't act dumb."

"She'd be upset," admitted Casey.

"You got that right. Rhiannon is not like that, Casey. She's not about revenge."

"What am I going to do?" asked Casey desperately.

"I don't know."

"What if something has happened to Taylor?"

"Yes, *what if?*" said DJ in a harsh tone.

"Will it be my fault?"

"What do you think?" asked DJ.

Casey nodded and looked down at her lap again. "I don't know what to do."

"I think you do," said DJ.

"Should I confess?"

"Let me ask you this," said DJ. "Which would be better — to confess now or get caught later?"

"What will they do to me?"

"I have no idea."

Now Casey was crying really hard, and DJ softened. "Look," she said as she reached for a tissue from her grandmother's desk. "You've made a really, really bad mistake, but if you try to cover it up and they find out ... well, it will only be worse. You understand that, don't you?"

Casey wiped her nose and continued to cry. "I'm so stupid, so freaking stupid. I don't know why I did that. It seemed so funny at the time ... just a little joke ... no big deal."

"Well, it's a big deal now, Casey."

"I know."

"And it could turn into an even bigger deal if something bad has happened to Taylor."

Casey looked at DJ with real fear now. "Do you think?"

"I don't know. But be realistic; it's a distinct possibility. I mean a girl like Taylor, a girl who is used to being comfortable, who likes her little luxuries, her clothes, her cosmetics, her silk pajamas ... to run off on her motorbike without taking a thing ... well, it does make you wonder."

"I wish I could undo what I did," said Casey. "If I could just turn back the clock, I swear I would be smarter this time. I wouldn't do it. It was so stupid ... so incredibly stupid."

"Well, you can't turn back the clock," said DJ. "All you can do is decide what's the right thing to do now."

"I know I need to confess," she said. "I'm just not sure I can do it on my own." She looked at DJ. "I wouldn't blame you if you said no, but would you come with me?"

DJ put an arm around Casey's shoulders now. "I'm totally mad at you for what you did to Taylor. But I still love you. You're still my friend. And if it'll help, I'll go with you."

Then DJ walked over and looked out the window to see that the police car was still parked in front. "In fact, maybe we won't have to go in. It looks like Detective Howard is still here. Do you want me to go get him?"

"I guess ..." Then Casey frowned. "Do you think he'll have to cuff me and take me away in the back of his car?"

"I honestly don't know."

"I suppose I deserve that kind of humiliation."

"Do you want me to get him or not?"

Casey nodded. "Yes, I just want to get it over with."

So DJ went to find the detective who was still talking to Mrs. Carter. He was telling her to make sure that all the girls stuck together in case there was a predator in the neighborhood. Then he asked when Taylor's parents would arrive.

"Her mother is flying out tomorrow," said Mrs. Carter as she twisted a handkerchief in her hand. She turned to DJ. "Did you need something, Desiree?"

"There was something else we wanted to tell Detective Howard," said DJ. "If you're done here, that is."

"I have no more questions." Mrs. Carter sighed dramatically. "This is all so very upsetting."

Soon DJ and the detective were back in her grandmother's office, and Casey immediately began to pour out her confession, with tears and all.

"I'm so sorry I did it," she said finally. "I can't believe how stupid I was." Then she actually held out her wrists like she expected to be handcuffed. "I really do deserve to go to jail. I'm ready."

He nodded in a somber way, but DJ thought she almost saw a twinkle in his eye. "Although you've just confessed to what might be considered libel, slander, or defamation of character, it will be up to Miss Mitchell to press charges. But I would like you to make a complete statement. Would you mind coming down to the station?"

"In your car?" she asked with fear-filled eyes.

"If you like. Or you can have someone bring you."

"Okay." She glanced at DJ. "Can you take me?"

"Sure."

"Right now?" asked Casey.

"I don't see why not."

So it was that DJ drove Casey to the police station and waited as she made her statement. DJ wondered if Casey needed an attorney, although nothing like that had been mentioned. And Detective Howard had made it clear that Casey was not under arrest.

"Do you think Taylor will press charges?" asked Casey as DJ drove them back to Carter House.

"I don't know, but I suppose it's a possibility . . . if she comes back at all."

Casey let out a long sigh. "I know you might not believe me, DJ, but I really do want Taylor to come back and be okay, even if it means she presses charges and I go to jail."

"I don't think you'd go to jail," said DJ as she pulled into the driveway. "Maybe juvenile detention though."

"Well, I don't care. I just hope that she's okay. I might not like her, but I don't want her to be hurt ... or dead."

DJ felt a shiver run down her spine. Even so, she tried to act nonchalant and confident as they got out of the car. "Taylor's not dead," she told Casey. "She's probably in the house right this very minute. Probably sitting next to my grandmother and asking her to pass the nonfat dressing."

But Taylor wasn't there. And she was still gone later that evening. All the girls had gathered in the living room, saying that they were going to watch a movie, but all they did was sit around and talk about Taylor, trying to think of where she'd gone and what had happened to her. And the more they talked, the more grisly and depressing the whole thing became.

Finally DJ stood and held up her hands. "Look, you guys, we can go around and around about this, but we're not doing anyone—not Taylor and not ourselves—a bit of good."

"She's right," agreed Rhiannon. "If we want to help Taylor we should pray."

"I don't know how to pray," said Eliza earnestly. "I mean, I've been to church with my parents occasionally, and I've heard my grandfather say grace before a meal, but that's about as far as it goes."

"I know how to pray," said Kriti, "but it might not be as you would pray."

"That's okay," said DJ with a confidence that surprised her. "I really don't know how to pray either. But I just do it anyway. I just tell God what I'm concerned about or what I'd like him to do and, even though I'm probably doing it all wrong, I think he's smart enough to sort it all out."

"I don't think there's a wrong way to pray," said Casey. "At least I think I heard our pastor say that once."

"Your pastor?" Eliza looked slightly shocked.

"Believe it or not, I did grow up in a Christian home," said Casey. "But that doesn't make me a Christian now."

"Oh." Eliza nodded with a slightly confused expression.

"Anyway," said DJ. "I think if we really care about Taylor, we should all be willing to pray for her—each in our own way. If anyone doesn't agree, she is free to leave."

Then to DJ's amazement, all five girls bowed their heads, and all five girls sincerely prayed for Taylor. And somehow DJ knew that if there was any way for Taylor to make it safely back to them, it would be the direct result of their prayers. She knew that God was listening. She just hoped their faith was big enough.

TAYLOR FELT BORED BEYOND BELIEF as she flipped through the limited cable channels on the grainy TV. One more rerun of *The OC* and she might have to pull out her hair or throw one of these ugly lamps or just scream. And that might draw the attention of the dimwitted reception clerk at this half-star hotel. Already, she felt worried that one of the workers, whether it was a maid or a room-service guy, might put two and two together and figure out who she was and what she was running from. After all, she had seen the local news more than once herself. Not only did they use a less-than-flattering photo of her, they had to go and mention that MySpace scandal as well. Talk about adding insult to injury. No wonder she wanted to lay low for a while. Who could stand such "lovely" publicity? On the other hand, who could stand this nasty old hotel for one more night? Not only did it smell like tuna fish and Lysol, the bed totally sucked and she'd already killed seven cockroaches by the minibar.

Even so, she wasn't ready to give up and go home yet. Home? She wanted to laugh at the mere thought of that word. As if she even had one. Yeah, right. She didn't have a "home" back in California where no one wanted her. And it certainly wasn't "home" back at Carter House where everyone hated her. Was there any such thing as home anyway? Or maybe just not for someone like her. And yet, it wasn't as if she had any other options right now either.

Although Taylor had always been a fighter and a survivor, she felt tired now. As she looked at the empty booze bottles, lined up like a worn-out army on the window sill, she felt like it was time to surrender. She was ready to wave her white flag and give up now. And hadn't that been her plan when she'd checked into this little hellhole? Her sole consolation for all she'd suffered? She'd even imagined the news report—how they'd discovered her body laid out neatly on the hotel bed—how she'd been fashionably dressed, every hair in place, even wearing makeup. She'd even purchased a bottle of pills, just in case she had the nerve to carry out her little exit plan. Of course, she'd also purchased her bag of booze, just in case she didn't. But that was gone now. And it was raining outside. And, really, why shouldn't she just end this thing?

Seriously, she wondered as she studied the depressingly dingy hotel room, what difference would it make if she checked out? Permanently. Who would really care? If anything, they'd probably all get together—her family and her so-called friends—and they'd probably throw a great big party. They would wear colorful party hats and blow noisemakers as they celebrated her demise. Perhaps they'd even sing that old *Wizard of Oz* song—"Ding, dong, the witch is dead ..."

But each time she played out this death-by-choice scenario, she had to face the big question—what came next? Because as badly as she wanted to escape all this—this pain of being unwanted, of being unloved—she was afraid to take that final step. And she had this strong sense that something deep inside of her didn't really want to die. She wasn't even sure how to explain it—or what it meant. But perhaps the truth was that she didn't want to cease to exist. She didn't want her life—no matter how pathetic—to be snuffed out like that. *Finis.*

And so Taylor considered doing something extremely out of character—something she hadn't done in years. It was something her grandmother had taught her to do, back before she'd died when Taylor was ten. "Don't you ever forget that it's your lifeline," Grandma had told her many a time. "And you hang onto it, Taylor girl, hang onto it for dear life." But the years passed, and Taylor had loosened her grip on it, and little by little, she had allowed the lifeline to slip from her grasp until it had vanished completely. She wasn't even sure if she could reach for it now.

But she decided, for Grandma's sake, to give it a try. And just to show she was in earnest, she kneeled down on the nasty matted-down carpet next to the bed.

"Dear God," she prayed. "If you're there ... if you still care about me ... I need some help. *I really, really need some help.*" And then she buried her face into the prickly polyester surface of the smelly bedspread and sobbed.

HomecominG queen

carter house girls

 meLODY
carLson

bestselling author

Read chapter 1 of *Homecoming Queen*, Book 3 in Carter House Girls.

DJ JUMPED AT THE SOUND OF SOMEONE opening her bedroom door. It was well past midnight and the house had been quiet for at least an hour now. The floor creaked as the intruder slipped into the room. With a pounding heart, DJ wondered if she should scream for help or simply play dead. Without even breathing, she peeked over the edge of her comforter just in time to see her long-lost roommate quietly closing the door.

"Taylor!" cried DJ as she threw back the covers and leaped out of bed. "Where on earth have you been?" Taylor, the tall dark-haired beauty, had been missing for days without a trace.

"Shh!" Taylor held a finger to her lips and then shirked off her leather jacket. It appeared to be soaking wet, and she dropped it to the floor with a heavy thud. "Don't wake up the whole house."

"We *should* wake them," said DJ. "I mean everyone's been freaking over you. We should tell my grandmother that you're back and—"

"Tomorrow," said Taylor as she unzipped her jeans and peeled them off. "It's late now. I just want to grab a hot shower and go to bed. No fuss."

"But what about the police and the—"

"Seriously, DJ. I am dead tired." Taylor scowled as she tossed the soggy jeans next to the jacket on the floor. "We'll sort it out tomorrow. I promise."

"But the others will be so relieved to—"

"I *mean* it, DJ," hissed Taylor. "Shut up and go back to sleep!" Then, acting like it was *no big deal*—like everyone in the entire town hadn't been freaking over her disappearance—Taylor slipped into the bathroom and quietly but firmly shut the door.

DJ felt slightly enraged. Wide awake and full of questions, she wanted to go in there and confront her roommate. She wanted to demand answers and explanations for this crazy missing act that had put everyone in Carter House on high alert all week. Who did Taylor think she was, anyway?

DJ could hear the water in the shower running and, remembering Taylor's determined look, DJ got back into her bed. It probably did make more sense to sort this whole thing out by the light of day. And although she was seriously irritated at Taylor's nonchalance, she was also hugely relieved that the girl was back. DJ remembered how these past two evenings, she and the other Carter House girls had gathered and actually prayed—each in her own way—that Taylor would make it back safely. And now, just like that, Taylor was here—and it seemed that she was just fine. Or as fine as a girl like Taylor could be. Anyway, it did seem that God really had been listening!

"You're kidding?" said Rhiannon after DJ told her the news the next morning. They were in Rhiannon's room, whispering. "Taylor's back? Is she here right now?"

"Yep." DJ nodded as she closed the bedroom door behind her. It was still early, but she had to talk to someone. And Rhiannon was the world's best listener. "She got in late last night and she's still asleep. Where's Casey?"

"In the bathroom." Rhiannon pulled her blue bathrobe off the end of her bed and wrapped it around her shoulders. "Did Taylor say where she'd been?"

"No. But she was soaking wet when she came in so I can only assume she rode home on her Vespa."

"Yeah. It was pouring down rain last night."

Rhiannon knocked on the bathroom door, calling out Casey's name. "She's got to know," Rhiannon said to DJ as they waited.

Casey emerged, wrapped in a towel with her short wet hair sticking out in all directions. She stared curiously at DJ. "What's up?"

"Taylor's back."

Casey's already large brown eyes now grew huge. "She's back?"

"Yep." DJ quickly filled her in on the late night arrival.

"And she's okay?"

"As far as I can see. She's asleep right now."

"Did you tell her ... about me? I mean, that I'm the one who did the MySpace thing?"

"No. She wouldn't even let me talk to her."

Casey sank into the window seat and slowly shook her head. "I guess this is when the stuff hits the fan, huh?"

"I don't know." DJ glanced nervously at Rhiannon, hoping she could say something encouraging.

"It's going to be okay," Rhiannon said to Casey in a soothing tone.

"How can you say that?" Casey looked at Rhiannon and then DJ. "I committed a crime! Libel and slander!" It was true. Casey had posted faked pictures of Taylor on a website and then put up signs at school so everyone they knew would look at them.

"No one is prosecuting you," said DJ.

"Not yet. But that could all change today." Tears slid down Casey's cheeks. "I can't believe I was so stupid."

"None of us can believe it," said DJ.

"It seemed like a great idea at the time," said Casey, wiping her nose on the edge of her oversized towel. "I thought I was being so clever—getting even with Taylor. She deserved it after how she hurt Rhiannon."

"Revenge never works," said Rhiannon.

"Tell me about it." Casey sighed.

"And worrying about it won't change anything," said DJ.

"That's easy for you to say." Casey stood. "I'm the one who could end up in jail."

"You're a minor," said Rhiannon.

"Okay, juvenile detention." Casey tightly shut her eyes. "That's even worse."

"That would only happen if Taylor presses charges," said DJ. "Remember what Detective Howard told us the other day?"

"Of course she'll press charges," declared Casey hotly. "She's probably already spoken to a lawyer. I'm toast."

"You don't know that," said DJ.

"I need to get dressed," said Casey quickly, heading back to the bathroom. "If I'm going down, at least I can have some clothes on."

"You're not going down, Casey." DJ made an attempt at a laugh, but she knew it sounded fake.

After Casey returned to the bathroom, Rhiannon looked at DJ. "Do you think she'll really have to go into juvenile detention?"

DJ shrugged. "It seems crazy, but I suppose it's possible. According to Detective Howard, she did break the law. Taylor has the right to press charges."

"We need to be really praying about this."

DJ nodded. "Yeah." She put her hand on the door handle and looked sympathetically toward the bathroom. "Well, I need to get ready for school. And I need to tell Grandmother what's up so she can notify the police."

"What about Taylor's parents? Do they know?"

DJ shrugged. "Guess that's Taylor's business."

DJ felt a mixture of emotions as she returned to her room. On one hand, she was relieved that Taylor was back—and safe. On the other hand, life would probably get complicated again. Casey was right; the stuff would be hitting the fan soon—and just after Casey had finally made an effort to fit in here at Carter House and after DJ's grandmother had decided not to send her home after all. That could all change now.

As DJ finished getting ready for school, she prayed for Casey. She wasn't even sure what to pray for, so finally she just asked God to bring something good out of this mess. She had no idea what that might be, but she felt certain that God could do it.

"You done in there yet?" asked Taylor in a groggy voice.

"Sure," said DJ as she opened the bathroom door up more fully. "I didn't know if you'd even be up yet. Are you planning on going to school today?"

Taylor shrugged and then pushed a dark strand of curly hair out of her eyes. Even after her late night, she still looked gorgeous. "I don't know."

"I'm going to let my grandmother know that you're back."

Taylor rolled her eyes. "Yeah. Whatever."

DJ controlled herself from saying something sarcastic back at her. She knew it wouldn't do anyone any good to get into a fight with Taylor today. If anything, she felt like she should be very placating, very kind and understanding. Maybe if she played her cards just right, she could induce a bit of Taylor's sympathy toward Casey. Possible, though unlikely.

"She's back, isn't she?" whispered Inez with dark, curious eyes. The housekeeper had stopped DJ on her way to Grandmother's room. "I saw her little green motorbike outside, and I know that means she's back."

DJ nodded. "Yes. She's back."

"Does this mean trouble, you think?"

"I don't know. Right now I just want to inform Grandmother."

"I'll tell Clara to set another place for breakfast."

"Thanks." Then DJ knocked on her grandmother's door. Although her bedroom was on the same floor as the girls, it was in the back of the house, with the stairway acting as a sort of buffer to the other rooms.

"Yes?" Grandmother opened the door, still wearing her rose-colored satin robe, as she peered blurrily at DJ. "What is it, Desiree?"

DJ quickly told her the news.

Grandmother blinked. "She's here now?"

"Yes."

"And she's all right?"

"She seems perfectly fine."

"Did she inform her parents?"

"I don't know. We haven't had a chance to really talk. I just wanted to let you know so you could contact the police and stuff."

"Yes. Yes, I'll get right to it." Grandmother smiled as she clasped her hands in front of her. "Oh, I'm so glad that she's back."

DJ nodded, but felt unsure.

"She's such a *beautiful* girl," said Grandmother.

DJ wondered what that really had to do with anything. "Well, yeah."

"And I have such plans for her."

"Oh." DJ got it. The old grooming-the-girls-to-be-models idea was poking its ugly head up again.

Grandmother put a thin wrinkled hand on the side of DJ's face. "Oh, it's not that you're not pretty too, Desiree. You most certainly are. But that Taylor—" The old woman smacked her lips like she were about to devour a piece of chocolate cream pie, or knowing her, more likely a carrot. "That Taylor—well, she has the makings of a real supermodel."

"Right." DJ stepped away now. "So, you will let the police and everyone know?"

"Oh, yes, of course." Grandmother nodded in a vague kind of way that suggested that she had already forgotten about Detective Howard and Taylor's parents, as if she had simply dismissed all of that as insignificant compared to the fact that Taylor had the "right stuff" to be molded into some kind of supermodel. Talk about delusional.

"And, Desiree," said Grandmother as DJ started to leave. "Please, tell Taylor that I'd like to see her in my room—before breakfast."

"Okay." DJ sighed.

"And don't slouch, dear," said Grandmother. Then she stood a bit taller herself, as if to show DJ how it was done. She held her pointed chin higher as she used the back of her fingers to give it a pat underneath, as if that might help the slightly sagging skin to tighten. "Good posture tells people that you believe in yourself, dear. It makes a good impression."

"Yeah, right." For her grandmother's sake, DJ stood a bit straighter, suppressing the urge to grind her teeth and growl as she walked back to her room. *Sheesh*. Sometimes DJ wondered if she was honestly related to that crazy old bat. DJ's mom, an intelligent and down-to-earth person, had been nothing like Grandmother. But then DJ's mom was dead. And DJ's dad didn't want to deal with a teenage daughter. Really, DJ knew she should be thankful for the old woman. But sometimes it was tough.

Carter House Girls Series from Melody Carlson

Mix six teenage girls and one '60s fashion icon (retired, of course) in an old Victorian-era boarding home. Add boys and dating, a little high school angst, and throw in a Kate Spade bag or two ... and you've got the Carter House Girls, Melody Carlson's new chick lit series for young adults!

Mixed Bags
Book One

Softcover • ISBN: 978-0-310-71488-0

Stealing Bradford
Book Two

Softcover • ISBN: 978-0-310-71489-7

Homecoming Queen
Book Three

Softcover • ISBN: 978-0-310-71490-3

Viva Vermont!
Book Four

Softcover • ISBN: 978-0-310-71491-0

Lost in Las Vegas
Book Five

Softcover • ISBN: 978-0-310-71492-7

New York Debut
Book Six

Softcover • ISBN: 978-0-310-71493-4

Books 7-8 coming soon!

A Sweet Seasons Novel
from Debbie Viguié!

They're fun! They're quirky! They're Sweet Seasons—unlike any other books you've ever read. You could call them alternative, God-honoring chick lit. Join Candy Thompson on a sweet, lighthearted, and honest romp through the friendships, romances, family, school, faith, and values that make a girl's life as full as it can be.

The Summer of Cotton Candy

Book One

Softcover • ISBN: 978-0-310-71558-0

The Fall of Candy Corn

Book Two

Softcover • ISBN: 978-0-310-71559-7

The Winter of Candy Canes

Book Three

Softcover • ISBN: 978-0-310-71752-2

The Spring of Candy Apples

Book Four

Softcover • ISBN: 978-0-310-71753-9

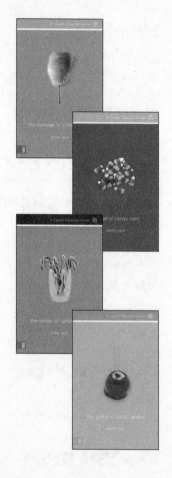

Pick up a copy today at your favorite bookstore!

Visit www.zondervan.com/teen

ZONDERVAN®
.com

Forbidden Doors

A Four-Volume Series from Bestselling Author Bill Myers!

Some doors are better left unopened.

Join teenager Rebecca "Becka" Williams, her brother Scott, and her friend Ryan Riordan as they head for mind-bending clashes between the forces of darkness and the kingdom of God.

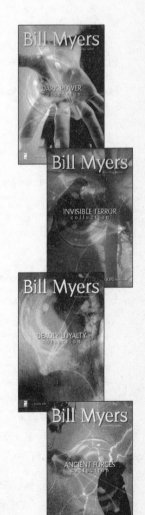

Dark Power Collection
Volume One
Softcover • ISBN: 978-0-310-71534-4

Contains books 1–3: *The Society, The Deceived,* and *The Spell*

Invisible Terror Collection
Volume Two
Softcover • ISBN: 978-0-310-71535-1

Contains books 4–6: *The Haunting, The Guardian,* and *The Encounter*

Deadly Loyalty Collection
Volume Three
Softcover • ISBN: 978-0-310-71536-8

Contains books 7–9: *The Curse, The Undead,* and *The Scream*

Ancient Forces Collection
Volume Four
Softcover • ISBN: 978-0-310-71537-5

Contains books 10–12: *The Ancients, The Wiccan,* and *The Cards*

Echoes from the Edge

A New Trilogy from Bestselling Author Bryan Davis!

This fast-paced adventure fantasy trilogy starts with murder and leads teenagers Nathan and Kelly out of their once-familiar world as they struggle to find answers to the tragedy. A mysterious mirror with phantom images, a camera that takes pictures of things they can't see, and a violin that unlocks unrecognizable voices ... each enigma takes the teens farther into an alternate universe where nothing is as it seems.

Beyond the Reflection's Edge
Book One

Softcover • ISBN: 978-0-310-71554-2

After sixteen-year-old Nathan Shepherd's parents are murdered during a corporate investigation, he teams up with a friend to solve the case. They discover mirrors that reflect events from the past and future, a camera that photographs people who aren't there, and a violin that echoes unseen voices.

Eternity's Edge
Book Two

Softcover • ISBN: 978-0-310-71555-9

Nathan Shepherd's parents are alive after all! With the imminent collapse of the universe at hand, due to a state called interfinity, Nathan sets out to find them. With Kelly at his side, he must balance his efforts between searching for his parents and saving the world. Will Nathan be reunited with his parents?

Book 3 coming soon!

Pick up a copy today at your favorite bookstore!

Visit www.zondervan.com/teen

ZONDERVAN®
.com

The Shadowside Trilogy by Robert Elmer!

Those who live in lush comfort on the bright side of the small planet Corista have plundered the water resources of Shadowside for centuries, ignoring the existence of Shadowside's inhabitants, who are nothing more than animals. Or so the Brightsiders have been taught. It will take a special young woman to expose the truth—and to help avert the war that is sure to follow—in the exciting Shadowside Trilogy, the latest sci-fi adventure from Robert Elmer.

Trion Rising
Book One

Softcover • ISBN: 978-0-310-71421-7

When the mysterious Jesmet, whom the authorities brand as a Magician of the Old Order, begins to connect with Oriannon, he is banished forever to the shadow side of their planet Corista.

The Owling
Book Two

Softcover • ISBN: 978-0-310-71422-4

Life is turned upside down on Corista for 15-year-old Oriannon and her friends. The planet's axis has shifted, bringing chaos to Brightside and Shadowside. And Jesmet, the music mentor who was executed for saving their lives, is alive and promises them a special power called the Numa—if they'll just wait.

Book 3 coming soon!

Pick up a copy today at your favorite bookstore!

Visit www.zondervan.com/teen

The Rayne Tour

by Brandilyn Collins and Amberly Collins!

A suspenseful two-book series for young adults written by bestselling author, Brandilyn Collins and her daughter, Amberly. The story is about the daughter of a rock star, life on the road, and her search for her real father.

Always Watching
Book One

Softcover • ISBN: 978-0-310-71539-9

This daughter of a rock star has it all — until murder crashes her world. During a concert, sixteen-year-old Shaley O'Connor stumbles upon the body of a friend backstage. Is Tom Hutchens' death connected to her? Frightening messages arrive. Paparazzi stalk Shaley. Her private nightmare is displayed for all to see. Where is God at a time like this? As the clock runs out, Shaley must find Tom's killer — before he strikes again.

Coming May 2009!

Last Breath
Book Two

Softcover • ISBN: 978-0-310-71540-7

With his last breath a dying man whispered four stunning words into Shaley O'Connor's ear. Should she believe them? After two murders on the Rayne concert tour, Shaley is reeling. But she has no time to rest. If the dying man's claim is right, the danger is far from over.

Coming October 2009!

Pick up a copy today at your favorite bookstore!

Visit www.zondervan.com/teen

ZONDERVAN®
.com